SUNFLOWER

A NOVELLA

ZAC CANNON

This is a work of fiction. Any similarities to actual persons, living or dead, or actual events, is purely coincidental.

The following contains material unsuitable for some audiences, including scenes some may find troubling or triggering. Discretion advised.

Edited by Sarah Ford

Cover artwork featuring contributions by
Kes Rodgers & Jaret Walen

Cover photography by Jess Cannon

Cover design by the author

DEDICATED TO
ALL THE WEIRDOS & LOVERS
WHO HAVE INSPIRED & ENCOURAGED ME
TO SEE THE BEAUTY IN THE MADNESS

So far from home
So far from here
With a little bit of hope
They see a little light appear

So far from home
So far from here
Sunflower alone
Sunflower disappear
Oh my God, what have they done

CODESEVEN

Will you levitate
Up where the angels inhabit?
Will you levitate
Where I won't reach you?

SLEEP TOKEN

The primordial sound, echoing out
Existence grows from itself, echoing out
What you seek, the obsolete
The answers are of no use to you now
Echoing out

THE CONTORTIONIST

ONE

Ayman worries the world might end before he accomplishes much more than fantasizing about kissing a real girl, and all his father seems to care about are the stupid fingerprints on the stupid door.

He spritzes the glass with cleaner, daydreaming of phantom lips. Wads of paper towels make frustrated noises against the glass as he takes the smudges to task.

His family's convenience store is dark. There's been no power for the past couple of hours, during which the store's shelves were picked over, refrigeration units sparse.

A candle bearing the image of some saint his poor mother has prayed to a lot the last few days burns low on the counter, behind which stands his father, Hafiz, an intimidating and broad Jordanian man.

Hafiz watches the boy work; he watches the candle burn. Yet, even with his stature and years, he is not immune to his imagination's anxious thoughts and misgivings.

Out of the corner of his eye, permitting little more than the peripheral, he keeps tabs on the boy's progress and the sky.

Up there. Constant. Always stalwart, but now threatening.

For a moment, Ayman's gaze slips past the knuckles of his hands; the oily smears he works hard to eliminate, and toward the heavens.

It's not the storm or the rain. Despite the chores and daydreams, it's still there; what looks like an angry bruise behind the clouds.

Hafiz notices his son's gaze.

"Ayman?"

Too late.

Just a glimpse of that slithering, pale light cutting through the atmosphere sends adrenaline coursing through the boy. It starts warm in his chest, spreading through his arms and legs before catching up to his thoughts.

"Ayman!"

His father's sternness jars him back to reality.

Hafiz watches him work his fear out through his arms up and down motions, both welcoming the distraction and squeaky solace of the menial labor.

From outside the store, a mirror image of the boy's face. His eyes are half hidden behind a hastily made cardboard sign that's been duct taped to the door.

Written in thick, quick scrawl: *KNOCK! NO PWR!*

Then, as if added on second thought: *$ ONLY $*

Ayman's attention is stolen again as a stranger hops the low wall bordering the lot, making a beeline for the store.

The boy drops his paper towels and slides back first into the shadows. His hand finds a baseball bat just as the stranger tries the locked door.

A couple of quick knocks on the glass follow.

"Hello?" asks a muffled voice.

Ayman cautiously peeks over a rack to the outside. He looks at his father, who reaches slowly behind the counter and nods to the boy.

A key inserted, deadbolt twisted.

Hafiz looms, watching as Ayman shrinks back into a corner, gripping the bat at his side.

A figure shuffles inside, a man, barely more than a silhouette in a rain-soaked hoodie. The beam of a flashlight darts here and there, following the trail shoppers blazed before him.

Past the picked-over shelves, he makes his way to the treasure he's hunting for: an ice cream chest.

They watch as the stranger slides open the chest and throws back his wet hood.

Hafiz relaxes a little at the sight of him, just your average, unremarkable American male barely in his thirties, if that. His voice is friendly enough, but Hafiz remains vigilant. He's been fooled before.

"Crazy, huh?" the stranger remarks.

He talks, continuing to dig through the chest, shaking a few cartons to the unfortunate sound of melting ice cream.

"Storm knocked your power out, too? Or did the city cut it? Mine went down sometime last night. Not sure. A real mess, though."

At the bottom, nearly out of hope, he finds two not quite thawed cartons.

He lifts them with a smile and places them on the counter in front of the large, quiet man.

"Guess this'll have to do?"

"Cash only."

"Yeah, yeah. I saw your –"

He digs in his wallet.

"Twenty dollars," the big man behind the counter says flatly.

"Twenty?"

Behind the counter, Hafiz seems to grow even taller and broader.

"Sure. Yeah," the young man says, nearly dropping a wad of folded bills. "Can't blame you."

Hafiz watches as he slides the twenty onto the counter beside the ice cream. He takes it but doesn't open the register, looming.

Wisdom prevails as the man in the wet hoodie decides it's probably time to get while the getting is good. Sliding the ice cream into his arms, Hafiz watches as he nods politely.

Ayman is in motion, sliding the door back on its track enough for the man to slip through with the ice cream. Just as quick, he twists the deadbolt with a click, then removes the key and shoves it into his pocket.

Hafiz watches through the window.

The storm is picking up. The man pulls his hood back up and leans into the rain.

Behind the counter, he removes his hand from where it has been resting on a shotgun stock.

At the door, Ayman watches the man trudge off into the night. He grabs the glass cleaner, points it at the window, but lowers it.

In the sky, a dancing light like nothing he, nor anyone else, has ever seen pulses just above the clouds. It is beautiful and terrifying.

Flashlight under his arm, Sean makes his way up to the second floor while snuggling the ice cream close to his chest. Even in the windowless dark of the apartment complex's halls and stairways, he navigates the familiar turns of his route without thinking.

At the door to his apartment, he leans against the wall to awkwardly fish keys from his pocket while juggling the snacks.

Before he can manage, the door opens as if on its own. Even with her back to him, Sean recognizes the short woman exiting the apartment. He holds his breath, watching as she closes the door, startling her on purpose.

"Hey, Jules."

"Jesus, what the heck?!"

"You're coming out of my place!"

"Well, you … you're sneaking around like some kind of … storm bandit."

"That's what, that's what you're going with?"

They share a smile, something familiar between them.

He asks, "Is she still mad at me?"

"First that I'm hearing of it. What did you do?"

"I didn't … I … you know, sometimes you just say things at the wrong time the wrong way. This is my peace offering. You're missing out."

"Last ice cream in the city? No sir. I'm not getting between a girl and her cravings."

He notices the long, grey jacket hiding her otherwise colorful hospital scrubs. As dark as it is in the hallway, Sean is intrigued by how the material catches the ambient light in tiny dots and pinpoints. The fabric is dull, yet it refracts just so.

He reaches out to feel her sleeve.

"What's going on with the getup? Fancy nurse stuff?"

"Running late," she deflects. "It's new. Lots of new. New bus policy. New check-in policy. A lot of new in my world, but you got quite the new headed your way."

"Pretty weird to think about it for too long, considering everything else."

"Weird is just weird until normal can catch up. We're all just behind the curve."

"All … whatever this is?" He motions with the ice cream to the darkness that surrounds them. "Normal is taking its sweet time."

"Trick is to realize it's always weird, and we're only ever chasing normal, which often means we're chasing something else."

This time she motions to the dark hall around them.

"Grand scheme of things," she continues. "Crazy and weird are probably more common than whatever normal we daydream about."

"Kat opened the wine, didn't she?"

"It may have been posited that since she couldn't drink it, someone had to. I'm kidding. And there's nothing for you to fret over. The only thing you should worry about is taking good care of our girl! She's doing great! You guys are doing great!"

She starts to go, turning with a grin. "Give her more of my love and eat all of that! Enjoy it. For me! And I left you some toilet paper."

"Thanks?"

"Word on the streets: toilet paper will be as scarce as ice cream. Keep clean, kid."

"Weirdo."

"Storm bandit."

They exchange an awkward, one-shoulder embrace

He watches her turn the corner, the hollow sound of feet descending in the stairwell, before shuffling into the apartment.

With no electricity and no better option, Sean goes directly to the kitchen and tosses the frozen treats into the freezer.

"Excuse me?"

No acknowledgment necessary, Sean retrieves one of the cartons from the freezer and slides open a nearby drawer. He grabs a pair of spoons.

"What do you think that's for?" A young woman steps towards him, taking the ice cream and the spoons. "This is all mine, mister."

Kat, his lovely wife. She's a five-months-pregnant-kind-of-cute, exuding a kind of cozy but feisty mom-to-be energy. Confident and empowered. She rips the plastic wrap around the carton's lid with her teeth. He watches her slide a spoon in before relenting and handing him one.

She says, "Heard you talking about me."

"It's a little melty," he warns. "I'm sorry about earlier."

She answers with her mouth full.

"Perfect."

Sean lights the last of a half dozen or so candles of varying shapes, sizes, and scents throughout the small room. Kat sits in a gliding rocker with her feet on a stack of diaper boxes. She spoons ice cream from a carton perched on her burgeoning belly.

"What's that one?"

"This is," he answers, examining the candle's label. "Christmas Cookies."

"Not too bad with that fireplace one."

Sean shrugs. He sits on the floor across from her, inspecting the empty carton.

This corner of the room is slowly being transformed into a nursery space, evidenced by a nearly assembled crib, a dangling mobile, and many unpacked boxes of baby stuff.

Outside, the bass of a passing helicopter nearby and the pulse of that strange light in the window behind them.

Inside, they barely register anything outside of each other, the little room and the glow of mismatched candles.

"Gonna finish that one too?"

"If I choose," Kat says. "It's not like we can hold onto it."

"Julie said it might be the last ice cream in the city. At least the last ice cream for a while."

Kat pouts. "That makes me sad."

"At least they had something with chocolate in it."

"Eh, it wouldn't've mattered. What baby wants, baby gets."

"Which baby are we talking about? The big one, or the little one?"

"Does it matter? And, big? I am … petite."

"Petite, more like … potato."

She arches her back and foists her belly at him menacingly.

"Oh, my back," she wines. "I could go for some fries right now, for real."

She settles back into her chair and reaches beside her, pulling out a baby name book. Flipping open the book rekindles a recognizable row between them; a cold argument sparked back to life.

"Ready for more?" she asks.

"C'mon, we're having a good time," Sean grimaces.

He falls back onto the floor, grabbing a nearby pillow and shoving it onto his face.

"You're the one who gets all grumpy about it; just because you don't want to know if you're siring a little ... Lucas or ... Luna? Ew. No. Doesn't matter. Both of those, not the ones."

Kat leans over to snatch the pillow hiding his face, but she can't reach it.

"You know," she continues. "We already bought the sticker thing. It says baby on board. So you can bring me all the ice cream you can find, but I'll need you on board too."

"Hey, I'm totally on board," Sean says, peeking out from behind the pillow. "I'm ... I'm a 2x4."

"That is ... that is not correct."

"I mean ... do we need to –"

"We don't. You're right," Kat says, closing the book. "I will just name our child, boy or girl, after my Great Uncle, whose name was ... Baxley ... Fergus. He went by Fergie. Great Uncle Ferg."

"You're out of your mind and a terrible liar."

"You will adore little Baxley Fergus."

Sean gets up and stands by the window. The world surrounding them lies hidden in the unusual darkness of a powerless city at night.

Above them, an eerie calm.

He looks into the eyes of a mirror image of himself. Those eyes reveal feelings he's not ready to share with his wife or the alternate dimension version of his wife eating ice cream over his doppelganger's shoulder in the reflection.

"What do you think about all this?" he asks them both.

"Vague? Ambiguous?"

"I mean," he says, turning back to her, "Everyone's acting like it's the apocalypse."

"Eh, we've survived, like, what, at least three or four apocalypses?"

"Still, aren't you a little worried? I mean, it's not, like, scary, but, Still ... it could be."

"If you let it be. We'll be fine."

"Know so?"

She licks the last ice cream from her spoon and settles back with her feet up.

"What are we talking about?" she aks. "Spores from outer space? Are aliens coming to draw the energy from the core of the earth? A comet passing overhead turns us all into zombies; rotten hands reaching up from the grave? But, honey, listen, I can't think of anyone else I'd rather be ripped apart by a ravenous hoard of the living dead than you."

"That's just because they'd definitely eat you first. I'd be left to fend the hordes off all alone. And that would be way worse. Being alone."

"Aw. I'd still love you with all my unbeating, undead heart."

She snaps at him, barring her teeth.

Sean tells her she's delirious.

"And quite possibly sliding into a delicious choco-coma, she replies before grimacing at the bad news sh's just now remembered to bear.

"Speaking of brainless things that bite, eh, Jules asked me to check on the boys in the morning. Maybe walk them? Said something about maybe being stuck at the hospital a while."

"Ugh. That's why she gifted us the toilet paper, huh?"

"Sooner or later, being at the beck and call of a needy little gremlin? Kinda going to be a thing."

"I'm already at the beck and call of –"

"Watch it!" Kat says, brandishing her spoon at her husband.

"Fine, but I've got Roscoe. You can have the little turd."

"But Barry is such a cutie. Little Bear Bear."

"He sucks. Snaggletooth little … who names a dog Barry?"

"Fine, and if this is the end times, I promise we'll eat him first."

She puts the ice cream down and beckons him to her. He obliges.

"This right now, right here? Just me, you, a couch, and a carton of ice cream you're not sharing. This is all I'll ever need. Us."

"Us? No matter what," she comforts him. "Us doesn't go anywhere. Except … except maybe to bed, but you've got to help me up."

The middle of the night. Sean sits in a rocker while Kat sleeps in the bed in the opposite corner. The empty ice cream carton lays on its side on her bedside table.

Light creeps in from the crazy night sky as the electromagnetic storm raging in the upper atmosphere intensifies outside the window.

Sean rocks slowly, barely conscious of the motion, looking at the cell phone. It is about to go dead. He flips through pictures of the two of them. Smiling. Happy. Early days.

His scrolling leads to the frozen images of a video waiting to be played. He smiles to himself as he clicks it, quickly lowering the volume. College. Some karaoke bar. They are both singing a pop song from a decade ago. Sean is way off-key. Kat is drunk, but she is killing it. They're both barely more than children.

The phone blinks its last blink.

It is dark.

And quiet.

He can feel those moments and memories from just a few precious years ago slipping away. Fading. A thunderous boom erupts outside as a nearby power transformer explodes! Sparks cascade across the way.

The windowpane, as well as most of the apartment complex, is rocked. The mobile trembles. Some cutesy baby art falls off the wall and crashes to the floor.

Kat rolls over in bed, struggling to sit up, and Sean is there to comfort her.

"You're ok. It's nothing. Just, I think something blew up. Like, electrical."

"Blew up? What?"

"It's the … the storm."

"Where were you?"

"Up. Just up. Thinking."

"No more. No more up. No more thinking."

They slide in bed together, snuggling.

His hand slides around her, past her belly, finding her breast. She forces it back down to her stomach. Her hands keep his in place. Then, against him, she closes her eyes, sleepy.

"No more up."

"No more."

Soon she's back asleep fast.

He moves his hand from underneath hers.

Off her belly.

He rolls onto his back in the dark and stares at the white ceiling.

Sleep is distant.

SUNFLOWER

TWO

The door glides open into Julie's quiet apartment. Kat eases inside. Sean moves in slowly behind her, scanning. Waiting.

The door clicks shut behind them, and from the back of the apartment, two beasts of wildly divergent size come bounding into the room full of spastic canine energy.

Sean braces himself against the pelting of tails and toenails.

Kat squats to greet their furry neighbors.

Roscoe, the older of the two dogs, a goofy-looking hound, slows himself. A low, welcoming bray gurgles from his saggy throat.

A weird-looking mutt with a Napoleon complex bares his crooked teeth and growls. Sean gives him the stink eye and flips him off.

"Stop it, Sean!"

The mutt, Barry, yields to the touch of his apologetic savior. He's on his back, getting his belly scratched by Kat in no time.

Between the fog and the drizzle, the gorgeous glow of the impressionistic morning sun catches in the moisture that wraps around them in a dream in which they're the only real characters.

Well, besides their hairy companions.

Kat nearly drops her small umbrella as she's tugged along. She hands one of the leads to Sean after he finishes shrugging his trusty hoody over his head.

As the foursome ventures away from the apartment complex, the soundtrack is the patter of raindrops on vinyl and the click of four pairs of long toenails on the sidewalk.

They weave through a trail cutting through a shared green area. Two wooden benches sit facing one another, old friends sharing a silent conversation.

A birdbath stands nearby, its water still.

The roosts and boxes affixed to several tree trunks surrounding the space seem oddly quiet. Vacant.

These details go unnoticed as the dogs pull their two chaperones along in hopes of rustling up a squirrel or two.

Barry stares into the bare branches overhead, urinating his disapproval of the tree-dwelling menaces that aren't menacing much this morning.

Sean and Kat lead the dogs out from under the low boughs of pine that hide a newer subdivision from the highway.

Many houses and townhomes sit uncopied, waiting for buyers, but those with signs of life seem quiet, people keeping to themselves indoors.

The curiosity about the situation gets the best of him. Sean takes his first honest look at the morning sky through the clearing haze.

The sun peeks out. It could be a lovely day if normality were not already subtly betrayed by an already apparent yet indescribable otherness far overheard. So far away, one can ignore it, like most things, if you don't look too long.

So, he doesn't.

Instead, he focuses on keeping pace with the click-clack of walking dogs and his wife's smile over her shoulder at him.

Rounding a cul-de-sac, they pass a pair of neighbors loading up their vehicles. Given the time of year, it would be easy to assume they were going on vacation. This isn't that.

Roscoe stops to sniff one of their mailboxes.

Kat and Barry keep moving around the loop, so she doesn't notice as the older of the two neighbors exchanges a couple of boxes of ammunition for a handful of cash with his younger neighbor.

The older neighbor, pushing retirement age, shoves the money into his pocket and shakes the younger man's hand. He's only got a few years on Sean, a family man by the looks of his lawn.

Sean eavesdrops while Roscoe sniffs, both intruding.

"I really … you think this is …?"

"Just in case. We'll see you guys up that way. Try not to stop. A lot is going on everywhere."

They make eyes with Sean, the dog pulling at his leash. Their body language tells him this is none of his business. He nods and moves on.

Sean catches up with Kat, who picks up a baggie of Barry's poop a couple of houses down.

"Does it feel strange to you?" he asks.

"Feels like dog crap."

"No, I mean, this. All this. Like we're not in on the joke."

She watches his eyes dart around, looking at windows with blinds drawn and closed garage doors.

"A little, sure." She holds up the dog poop, shaking the bag like a disgusting maraca. "Distraction tactic!"

"You're so weird," he says, unable to resist a smile.

"You love it, and it worked," she says, kissing him on the cheek. "Oh, look at that. Your turn."

Sean turns to see Roscoe hunched over, back legs shaking, and eyes wide. "Why does he always look so uncomfortable?"

"He's making the same face you've been making all week. Constipated with angst."

She raises her eyebrows, and Sean opens a plastic baggie and crams his hand inside.

"You're just a comedian today."

"Someone's got to lighten the mood."

"Alright … but … what do they expect us to do? I mean, no phone? No internet? No power?! Just sit and, what, wait? Wait for somebody to tell us what's next. What to do? While we just –"

"Keep picking up the turds?"

"Yeah."

As they walk home with the dogs, soft and ineffable, cascading just barely visible above the clouds, an aurora.

While perhaps not unnatural, it is unusual and unnerving enough for anyone who might venture an eye.

Both dogs greedily scarf down kibble without a hint of etiquette as Kat refreshes their water bowls. Finally, she hands the bowls to Sean. Barry growls at his hand as he sets them on the tile floor before lapping at the water with his little, dumb tongue.

"Gotta pee," Kat tells Sean, hurrying past.

"We live down the hall."

"I. Am. Pregnant."

"You know, you're not going to be able to use that excuse forever."

"I'm not the one gnawing my fingers raw counting down the days, am I?"

She blows him a raspberry, bending to scratch Roscoe's ear before disappearing into the adjacent bathroom. Sean is surprised to find he's more than a little wounded by her jab. Stepping on the pedal of the trash can to deposit the poop bags provides an adequate distraction: an official-looking letter swims at the top of the rubbish.

He can see that the letterhead bears the name of the hospital where Julie works. It piques his curiosity enough to retrieve it. Sean scans the text across the top. It is intimidatingly bold.

He reads it out loud to the dogs as officially as he can, "Confidential! Divulging any information herein …."

His imitation fades as he follows the words on the page, growing less artificially serious as the nature of the communication becomes clear.

"What's that?" Kat asks.

"Didn't hear you wash your hands."

She rubs her hands through his hair and into his eyes.

"Stop, I'm trying to … it; it looks like some kind of affidavit. That what you call them? Maybe, like, an NDA? A non-disclosure –"

"I am aware of what an NDA is. Can't just toss those in the bin, though."

"I'm just saying it looks important. What do you think?"

He passes the letter to her. Kat begins reading nonchalantly. It doesn't take long for the letter's content to take her on the same journey from indifference to surprise to apprehension.

"This is," she hands the letter back to Sean, who doesn't seem to want to take it. "This is … I don't … there's HIPAA, but that's not this. How far did you get?"

"Far enough. I mean, there's not a lot of specifics."

He's been looking in the rubbish bin while she reads. He pulls out a plastic wrapper. There's a sticker with a UPC code and a black and white image of a man wearing the same strange jacket Julie was wearing. Sean scans the details: radiation protection/EMF shielding.

They take a seat on Julie's couch. Barry tries once, twice, three times to bound up and in between them. They thwart him each time, so he sulks away.

"Doesn't make sense."

"I mean, this is like something, what? Classified? It says, 'Talk about it, and you're gone.' Terminated."

They sit in silence for a moment. It's broken only by the awkward slurping noises of Roscoe licking himself, splayed out on the floor in front of them.

"I wish I could call Julie." She mimes picking up a phone. "Hey, friend, we were just reading your mail. Your classified inter-office communication."

Sean joins the pantomime. "Any top-secret information on the imminent, uh, alien invasion you'd like to share with your favorite neighbors from down the hall? We fed your dogs and picked up their poop. All of it."

They share the kind of dry, steam-letting laugh that only two people who have known each other a long time can. After some more reluctant silence, Sean clarifies, "It's probably not aliens."

"Probably not."

Kat walks over to the window, hand instinctively on her belly.

"See any spaceships?" Sean asks wryly.

She ignores him, taking in the view.

The last of the morning's beautiful Dreamsicle sky polluted with more of those little wisps pulsing high in the atmosphere.

"It says," she pauses. "It says that whatever is going on out there, up there … maybe it is serious. But like, lightning? More storms? Random, like, stuff exploding in the middle of the night?"

Sean joins her at the window.

"Even if someone gets hurt sometimes, it doesn't make the kind of people that make decisions like this worry," Kat continues.

"Remember those people we saw on our walk? They were packing up their cars?" Sean asks. "Looked like they were going on a trip somewhere?"

"They weren't."

"No. They were … let's just go home, OK?"

Kat turns her attention back to the world outside the apartment. "Maybe we should leave Julie a note?" she asks him. "Make sure Roscoe and Bare-Bare have water. Then, what if –?"

"I'm supposed to be the paranoid one," Sean says.

She receives his arms as they wrap around her from behind.

"I'm not paranoid. You said it, though, yeah? 'I don't know what they expect us to do. Just sit here and wait?' Is that what you want to do?"

It's pitch black in the parking garage underneath their apartment complex. Pack-laden, Sean guides Kat with his flashlight until they find a familiar sedan.

Kat buckles herself into the passenger side seat of their small sedan while Sean shrugs off their travel bags and tosses them into the back.

He hops in, pulling on his belt while cranking the vehicle.

"Alright," he asks. "Where to?"

"We're only supposed to go anywhere if it's an emergency."

Sean puts the car in drive.

"We get pulled over," he tells her, "We can say we're going to your parents' house."

"That's like a nine-hour drive."

"They don't have to know that."

Kat makes an exaggerated, exasperated gesture. "Shoot!"

"What?!"

"Should've brought the baby name book with us! We stopped at, what, L? No, K!"

Sean ignores her as he backs out of their numbered parking spot.

"So," he says, ignoring her and adjusting his mirror. "We just make it up as we go, or …?

Kat won't let it lie. She taunts him.

"There's, well, there's Kayden. Katy. Kingston. Karla. Kieran."

"There's also my favorite: Kissmybutt. I think it's Finnish."

She stretches feebly over the armrest to kiss him as the taunting intensifies. "Korbin. Kara. I think Kara means beloved or cherished."

"How about Kat? Which probably means, like, freakin' annoying."

They reach the street level, and Sean looks both ways.

They're the only traffic visible in either direction.

"I was named after the patron saint of scholars: Catherine of Alexandria. Did you know they tortured her to death on a spiked execution wheel? Instead of blood from her wounds, milk – a milk-like substance – poured from her body. So what does your name even mean?"

Sean looks ahead, ready to leave but letting her have her moment.

"I bet your name means," she continues. "It means, like, has no sense of fun. Or wet blanket. S for Sourpuss."

"First of all, Baxley Fergus IV," Sean retorts with a smile. "Your parents are psychos if they named you after Lady Milkblood. And, B, can we pick a direction if you're done?"

"I mean, are we thinking cozy motel for the night or likely to be back home by dinner?"

"Might as well go sleep in a tent in the woods if you're going to ask me to stay the night in some creepy motel with no power."

"That does sound like a horror movie."

The car slows a block away as they reach the intersection where a familiar convenience store stands.

Kat notices Sean's look of concern and follows his gaze.

Outside the store, Hafiz and Ayman work to board up their family's business with large plywood panels. The glass on the door Ayman attempted less than eagerly to polish the afternoon before now kicked in.

Sean gives a light, passing wave from the driver's seat as they drive by. Ayman raises a hand to wave back, but his father minds the chore.

"Maybe we should turn around," he says. "Safety of our boring, quiet, dark living room … what do you think? Home, or not?"

"I think," she says, turning on the radio.

"You won't find anything," he tells her as she scans the airwaves.

Sure enough, it's mostly nothing. Static. Official sounding information about staying at home, staying off the roads. More than once in the half a minute, Kat scrolls the dial; they wince as she stumbles upon the ear-splitting squawk of the emergency broadcast transmission.

Maybe for the first time ever, Kat switches to the AM band on the radio. But, unfortunately, her luck doesn't seem much better until she eventually lands on something classic with a groove some brave soul was brave enough to send out on the airwaves.

"Drive," she tells him.

Their hands find one another as an air of lightness and adventure – and a taste of that elusive normalcy – permeates the space between them. In the rearview, outside the store, the promises of things falling apart.

THREE

It's not long before Kat's humming to the music in the passenger seat. The window is down—her outstretched hand dances in the breeze.

There's something about how her face lights up when she's in the groove. It starts in her eyes, moves to her smile, and shimmies through her arms and legs.

It's infectious.

"When I say The Classic, what comes to mind?" Sean asks her, grinning.

"So many things," she answers. "And then again, so many things don't come to mind because of The Classic."

"Good bar. Nothing stands out, though?"

"I did kiss Rachel Meadows in front of Dr. Schriever in hopes that he'd raise my grade after bombing that midterm in Calc our last year."

"Did it work?"

"I ... don't even know if it was Dr. Schriever."

"Yeah, good bar."

"I do remember something," she says playfully. "Someone."

"Yeah?"

"Uh-huh. This poor, sad boy. I don't know if he even liked beer, the way he was nursing it. Just ... just sinking like a stone trying to sing, what was it?"

"It was *Airplanes.* I was trying to do the rap part."

"You were trying."

They laugh as she mimics her version of what she remembers hearing the evening they first met.

"Then you," he says. "You rescued me."

"I did. I saved that poor little boy. Then I got him drunk and had my way with him."

"Here I am trying to reminisce."

"So am I," she says, coping a feel. "You wanna pull over?"

"Get out of here."

She lets the rhythm take her away in the seat beside him as she starts dancing and singing again.

She rescued him – rescues him – and he knows it.

Like the swell of a good song playing on the radio that loses its signal, their revelry is cut short when Sean is forced to yank the car to the shoulder as he narrowly avoids another vehicle stopped dead on the road.

Kat looks up from the nail she's been chewing on.

"What's up?"

"Don't know. Can't see."

Kat unbuckles and cranes her neck out the window.

"Doesn't look like an accident."

"Get your head in here, ya' loony!"

The traffic crawls forward. A half dozen cars are filing through a makeshift roadblock up ahead. On the far side, military personnel force the vehicles to the side of the road.

Sean watches them moving up and down the line, waving cars over, and talking on radios.

What is going on, and what are they wearing?

The soldiers move around in silver-flecked fatigues. Those who don't wear protective masks hugged to their faces have them dangling around their necks. All of them are well-armed.

Sean's anxiety is elevated as his brain connects the dots between the men and women milling about with guns and the fabric of the material Julie's scrubs were made of. What was it? Some kind of protection, but from what exactly?

He sits up, rigid. Cautious. Meeting eyes with the driver he nearly just rear-ended; Sean waves an apology before squeezing back into the queue.

Kat buckles back in beside him, giving it a quick, instinctual tug to check its functionality. She rolls her window up.

"Weird," they both say in tandem with the screech of brakes, tires on asphalt, and metal crunching.

The two of them barely have the chance to register anything at all.

Sean reactively throws his arm over his wife just as the car behind them bounces off their rear end.

It's not as bad as it could be. Both seat belts do what they're made for, locking on impact, but Kat's digs under her breast uncomfortably.

"Ah," she exclaims!

"What?!"

"My freakin' boob!"

"That's all?"

She reaches over and pinches his nipple through his shirt. "It hurt!"

"Stop! I mean, are you OK?"

"I … I guess."

She lifts the strap from where it is wedged between her chest and belly, massaging. Sean opens his door, slowly stepping onto the highway. She reaches to stop him, fighting to get untangled from the strap.

"Hey? Don't," she says.

He looks at the car behind him and gives the other driver a questionable thumbs up. The driver seems shaken as well but returns the gesture.

"Keep that on," he tells her. "Seriously."

Sean surveys. They were lucky: the rear end of their car had suffered minor damage.

He notices the same cannot be said for the Winnebago responsible for the accident. It is the last in a growing line, just a few vehicles back, having driven two or three cars forward. Its grill smokes and belches.

Sean turns back to the car, motioning again for Kat to stay put, and leaves her to investigate.

Kat flips down the vanity mirror just as Sean disappears out of sight. She strains in her seat, turning, but the blasted seat belt keeps her from maneuvering to a better point of view.

Overhead, despite being the middle of the day, the sky seems to darken, angry but beautiful as tendrils of aurorae bloom in the atmosphere.

The further Sean moves along the line of dinged vehicles, the more shaken up the people he encounters are.

One family has evacuated their vehicle and stands huddled at the side of the road. They gather in a circle, hands clasped, praying.

Nearly every vehicle he steps past seems loaded with, or bearing, luggage and other necessities.

Sean stops to help a couple tighten a ratchet strap that keeps a pod of suitcases attached to a car far too small. It's an incredible display, a juggling act, but nothing can top the next vehicle in line.

Sean is stunned.

What appears to be space blankets and tinfoil have been affixed – somehow – to the interior of an aging Buick. The mysterious driver sits obscured and barely visible through the holes they've cut out for visibility. Sean imagines a giant bag of Jiffy Pop inflated inside the vehicle, trapping the driver inside.

Though odd, more than curious, and a little comical, something whispers to Sean to keep moving.

An old station idles pinned between another vehicle and the Winnebago towards the back of the line. The driver of the station wagon, a frail-looking older man, is bleeding from his forehead.

Sean knocks on his window.

The frail man appears dazed, likely concussed.

Still trying to see, well, anything really, Kat is jostled as a trio of soldiers jog past their car towards the wrecked Winnebago and her husband.

Unlike the others, these three wear standard fatigues. The only thing out of place is the strange-looking belts around their pelvises.

Kat scrambles to watch where they're headed, determined but hindered.

Motivated and curious, even more so if she understood those weird belts were for gamma radiation protection, Kat gives in and unfastens her seat belt.

Sean tries the bleeding man's door. It's locked. The man inside is now unresponsive, draped over the steering wheel. Sean raps on the glass with his knuckles.

"Move away, please."

Sean turns to see one of the three soldiers. He's young. His smooth face is still a little heavy with late adolescent baby fat; he was likely walking through high school corridors less than a year ago.

The other two soldiers hustle past the end of the line, leaving him to stand eye-to-eye with Sean. Those eyes betray the young man's lack of genuine experience; his voice barely hides his fear.

"Return to your vehicle, sir."

Another soldier, an officer by the looks of the insignia embroidered on her jacket, dodges behind the Winnebago to stop any more oncoming traffic.

Sean watches her reach for the driver's side door of the Winnebago just as it opens, and a confused-looking man stumbles out of it.

"Sir, can you walk?" the officer asks.

The man nods, standing on wobbly legs.

"Are there more people in the vehicle?"

Sean watches the man nod again.

"I'm going to need to get you out of the road before we can assist you."

Sean jumps as glass is shattered directly behind him!

The baby-faced soldier has broken the back window of the bleeding man's vehicle with a spring-loaded window punch. Sean watches him reach through, avoiding the remaining glass to unlock the driver's door.

A camouflaged military transport arrives from beyond the roadblock with more military personnel. The Transport Operator begins speaking through a PA mounted on the vehicle.

"Attention! Please. For your safety and to assist us in assisting you. We need you to remain in your vehicles or return to them immediately. If you or someone in your party requires emergency medical assistance, we will soon provide transport to a nearby medical facility.

"All remaining travelers: you will be provided instructions for our departure. Once we have cleared the roadway, you will collect your possessions, lock your vehicles, and board one of the transports. Next, you and your party will be taken to a nearby emergency shelter for observation."

"Sean?"

He turns toward her familiar voice and finds his beautiful, pregnant wife standing alone on the side of the road. More striking is the sky above the trees behind her: a cascading light dances around her as the atmosphere changes.

"Again," the Transport Operator continues over the PA. "We need you to return to your vehicles immediately."

A hand grabs Sean's shoulder.

The baby-faced soldier. He's trying to get the bleeding man out of the vehicle and onto the ground.

"Give me a hand?" the soldier asks.

Sean helps, slowly lowering the man's head to the asphalt as the sound of boots crunching on pavement signals the arrival of another soldier. This new arrival, a lean man carrying his rank and reputation in his posture, looks at Kat sternly. Sean doesn't much care for it.

"Excuse me! Miss? Go back to your vehicle. Now!"

Something inside Sean unfurls. He forces his way between the soldier and his wife.

"Don't talk to her like that."

Kat is surprised by this display of chivalry. It's not that Sean is a pushover; this kind of confrontation is not his style. On the contrary, she swells with something like pride, the object of his loyalty, but these men are soldiers with weapons.

Her eyes fall to their sidearms.

The entire scene fails to play out any further.

They are all caught off guard as a nearby engine roars to life. It's the tin foil-lined Buick, the driver's eyes hardly visible through the makeshift porthole in his space blanket submarine of a conspiracy mobile.

The officer ignores Sean completely and turns.

Hands readying his weapon, he approaches the vehicle as it revs.

There's not much room to maneuver, but the driver is determined. He attempts to squeeze the big car along a narrow path that exists only in his imagination between the others stopped on the roadside and the slope of the shoulder's shallow embankment. The attempt fails. The vehicle's tires spin. Stuck.

All the while, the encroaching luminescence.

Reasonably bewildered, Sean and Kat watch as the officer and another female soldier approach the vehicle and extricate the driver roughly.

Forced to the ground with a knee in his back, one of the soldiers pulls what looks like an aluminum balaclava from the now frantic and irate man's head.

His eyes are wide; his face shadowed in stubble, and his hair a tangled nest of madness.

"You're going to get us all killed," he bellows. "No! Stop! No!"

Staggering, Kat steps back, her hand searching for Sean's.

Instead, tendrils of dazzling energy arrive from nowhere and everywhere, wrapping around Kat's body.

A pulse.

A shutter signals a kind of confusion coursing throughout her body. Her senses leave her; her legs fail her.

Sean dives for his wife as she collapses to the ground at the roadside.

FOUR

Sean cradles Kat's head in his lap. She lays unconscious as they bounce in the back of the covered military transport. The elderly man with the head wound and a few other banged-up travelers console themselves or sit silently along the benches bolted under the covered bed, shocked and vacant.

Behind the wheel, the Transport Operator navigates back through town. One of the young soldiers from the roadside says something official sounding over his radio, but it barely registers as actual words.

Sean is only focused on his wife. He gently traces a painful-looking, discolored bruise on the back of her hand to where it disappears under her sleeve at the wrist.

The transport rolls past the convenience store Sean so recently visited, unconcerned with the looters who have gathered there. He watches out the back when they pass as a masked man attempts to pry off a piece of plywood while others are vandalizing the boarded-up storefront with spray paint and wanton destruction.

The hospital is on lock down. Emergency lighting only. The halls are dim. Anything nonessential? Non-operational.

The baby-faced soldier from the roadblock accompanies Sean through the double doors as a team of medical professionals swarm them.

As they move Kat to a gurney for transport, the young soldier grabs Sean's arms. Sean is taken aback by the genuine concern in his eyes.

"I hope you're both alright," the soldier says earnestly.

Then, he's gone.

Sean watches as the team swarms his wife, checking vitals and other routine things. His observation and thoughts are interrupted by the admitting nurse.

"I need to get some information from you," the nurse says.

He barely notices her as he watches his wife lying unconscious, unresponsive, only a few feet away. Time seems to be moving in fits and starts.

"What is your relationship to the patient?"

"Husband. Um, wife. Partner. We're married."

"Any allergies?"

"I don't ... I ... not that I know of."

"And how far along is the pregnancy?"

They're interrupted from this somewhat typical routine as more nurses, accompanied to Sean's surprise by two armed guards, arrive and take over.

One of the new nurses takes the admitting nurse aside. Only a few words are shared between them, and the admitting nurse quickly removes the first team from the situation.

Sean tries to get someone's – anyone's – attention.

"What's going on?"

"She's being moved to another unit," the new nurse tells him.

"To a room? To where?"

"You can follow us for the moment if you'd like."

They work quickly and efficiently, and the bed is moving before Sean has had the time to react. They're down the hall, which seems to be collecting patients.

"What about a doctor? When can we see a doctor?"

"You will be able to speak to someone once we get a clear assessment."

"Assessment of what?"

"Has your wife experienced any nosebleeds? Complained of headaches? Dizziness?"

"No, I mean ... she's been ... asleep since –"

They reach an elevator. An armed guard stops him abruptly and without courtesy. "This lift is for staff and patients."

A kind nurse looks him in the eyes with gentleness despite their hurry.

"Down the hall, turn left. We're going to the third floor. Someone will assist you when you get there."

"I'm going to stay with her," Sean tells them.

"Afraid not. You'll need to move, sir," another armed guard demands.

The first hospital guard accompanies the nurses and his wife in the elevator while the second remains stationed at the doors.

Sean can do nothing as the elevator's doors retract.

He looks at the elevator for an awkward moment until the guard motions for him to head down the hall.

Sean notices how quiet the hospital has gotten when he reaches the other bank of elevators. Or is it just his anxiety playing tricks on him?

He pushes the call button. Waits.

He presses it again.

Again.

And again.

Nothing is happening, and it is not happening way too fast.

Panic sets in because the elevator is not coming!

Rapid fire, his thumb finds the call button.

Nothing!

What has it been, fifteen seconds? It feels like fifteen minutes!

Sean turns back the way he came, frantic, and nearly collides with a gray-haired woman who has clearly been crying recently.

"Excuse me," he apologizes.

"These elevators aren't working," she tells him. "None of them are if you're not wearing a nametag or a badge. My sister is up on five. You'll have to take the stairs."

She points him toward a map on the wall.

Labeled just around the corner: stairs.

"Thank you," he tells her. "Thank you."

Sean makes it up the next two floors without responding to the pain in his legs or lungs, stopping only at the door marked Three South to rest before grabbing the handle. He is sure it won't turn. It does.

The door opens onto an empty landing. Sean jogs to the vacant information desk just down the hall. It is flanked by solid steel doors.

Sean tries to look through the narrow windows on the door, but the opaque glass thwarts him. Like the elevator, he presses the intercom button on the wall repeatedly. Finally, he peers into the tiny camera lens housed above it.

Nothing.

Frustrated. Panicking. *What is happening?*

"Please take a seat. Someone will be with you momentarily," says a voice over the intercom, startling Sean.

Sean's posture betrays his frustration.

"I assure you your patience and compliance will be to your benefit. Have a seat, please," requests the metallic-sounding voice again.

Sean finds a row of lightly padded but uncomfortable looking chairs. In defiance, he opts to lean against the wall instead. He double-checks to ensure he's in front of the camera lens, folding his arms over his chest.

He waits with as little patience and compliance as he'll allow.

Huffing.

Puffing.

Making 'come on with it now' eyes.

The landing remains quiet. Sterile. Lifeless.

Still, he waits.

Just when he's about to lose his composure, an audible clicking sound followed by the whir of a locking mechanism and the hiss of releasing air.

The doors on the opposite side of the desk glide open, and a tall, very tired-looking doctor steps out. He's accompanied by one of the nurses and the armed guard from the elevator. All three are gowned in protective coveralls, not identical, but similar enough to what Julie left their apartment in.

"Mr. Beckett? Sorry for the inconvenience," the tall man says. "I'm Doctor Hirsch. Please, come with us."

"Where's Kat?"

"She's resting. Stable. And your …" Doctor Hirsch looks down his nose and checks his chart. "Your daughter appears to be doing as well as we can hope."

Sean's noticeably dazed, but no one seems to register it; the statement knocks out what little wind is left in him.

The nurse hands him a long, pullover smock made of the same weird material as the coveralls they all wear.

"If you would please put this on, you can follow us this way."

Once the door closes, Sean hears the same click, whir, and whoosh. An airlock. This may have recently been a standard hospital wing, but no longer. They pass through another glass door, and Sean notes that the walls and many surfaces have been covered in foil lining, more and varied kinds if shielding.

The wing is open, beds along the walls separated by strips of the same foil material and similar privacy curtains. A nurse's station acts as a busy hub in the center.

Doctor Hirsch speaks in a hurried but direct manner while leading.

"Your wife, Mrs. Beckett, Katherine, has been exposed to, well, we're all unsure of the specifics, in all honesty. This unit has been dedicated to cases like hers. As you can see, as incidents have increased, so have our precautions.

"Preliminary exposure to what is being called colloquially 'the source' is generally followed by a period of unconsciousness akin to slow-wave sleep. Upon waking, initial side effects include weakness, fatigue, headaches, confusion, and frequent nosebleeds. We're treating these patients, as we'll continue to treat your wife, symptomatically to the best of our ability, but we just –"

"You don't have any idea? You don't know what's going on with them? You don't know what it is? What did this?"

They stop outside a drawn curtain, voices lowering.

"Like I said, Katherine is stable. You can see her. However, I need you to understand something, Mr. Beckett."

"Sean."

"The patients who have been with us the longest … it's like this everywhere as far as anyone can tell. D.C., San Francisco, Dallas; all over Europe, Russia. The more often they're in these sleep states – and the frequency and duration will increase – the longer it seems they stay that way. We have a handful of patients who are essentially in a coma. I bring this to your attention for several reasons, the chief being that your wife's situation may eventually dictate the course of action."

"The baby. What about Kat, though? Will she be alright?"

"Complications with the pregnancy could arise. Go see your wife. I will have someone check on you– the three of you – very soon. In the meantime, please wear that over your clothes."

Consulting a clipboard, he begins to walk away.

Sean stops him. "How long have these people been here?

"The earliest case was brought to our attention on Thursday."

"That's ... less than a week."

Sean turns at the sound of a curtain sliding back.

There she is, Kat.

She's awake but woozy. A couple of the machines she's connected to beep, vitals mostly. But, the most disconcerting is the electroencephalogram attached to her head. A monitor next to her displays readings that mean nothing to Sean.

When Kat sees his face, though, her whole demeanor changes. She manages a smile. Nothing matters more.

He shrugs the weird tunic over his head and rushes to her, kissing her hard on the lips. She begins to cry but continues to smile through the tears and a couple more kisses.

Their reunion is interrupted by the arrival of a familiar nurse. Julie. She seems genuinely happy to see them but off. Leary. She keeps her distance and her voice down as she enters.

"Mrs. Beckett?" she asks.

The three of them are more emotional than they'd like to be.

"Word gets around," Julie says. "I hoped it would just be a coincidence, the names ... you're here, though. You are. How ya feeling, girlie?"

"Thirsty," Kat responds; her hoarse voice is the evidence of her answer.

"I can do something about that. What about you?"

"I'm good now. Thanks, Jules," Sean tells her.

"Let's feign a little ignorance for the time being, OK? Not come off as too familiar?"

She seems on edge as she walks out, presumably to get water or something. This would bother Sean if he had the wherewithal to consider anything besides the woman in the hospital bed that has given him quite a scare.

He squeezes his wife's hand, asking, "You ok?"

"I am now."

"I guess things got weird, huh?"

"I'm sorry. I should've stayed in the stupid car."

"No, no, no. None of that."

"I was worried about you."

"You're not allowed to, not anymore. Not right now."

He pulls a chair over to her. He leans back, watching the rise and fall of her baby bump under the hospital blankets.

"They told me about her," he confesses. "I guess we can narrow the list down. We still on K?"

"Yeah, but I don't really like any of them."

He kisses away another runaway tear.

"No K's then."

Julie comes back in with a plastic cup full of ice water. She hands it to Sean, and he guides the straw to Kat's lips.

"Not too much too fast."

Kat wants to drain the cup but uses restraint. She's reasonably refreshed as both color and cheer return to her face.

"What on earth are you two wearing?"

"It's supposed to shield us. Same as all this."

Julie motions to the sheeting that surrounds them.

"Shield you? From what?" asks Kat.

"From a type of radiation. Gamma. Some other precautions."

Kat looks more and more concerned.

"What's radiated?"

"To some degree," Sean adds. "Everything. Radio waves. Microwaves. The light we see. But that's not what this is all about, Julie?"

The curtain is pulled back unceremoniously. A young aide wearing even more protective gear enters, pulling a cart with more equipment.

"Mrs. Beckett," Julie says, affecting her most professional tone. "We're going to continue monitoring a few things. Lisa will also be taking some blood. It shouldn't take more than a couple minutes. I'm just going to step outside with your husband for a second."

She looks at Sean and motions for him to follow her out.

FIVE

Julie holds the curtain for Sean. He catches a glimpse of his wife before it closes behind them. Kat seems far more concerned with the aid's medical implements than his brief absence.

"The bathrooms are just this way."

Julie takes him by his arm, leading. He follows her, questioning the subtle subterfuge. As soon as they're clear of idle eyes, Julie pulls him into an unoccupied room. She hugs him tightly.

"It's OK, Jules."

She hushes him, keeping her own voice down. "Oh, dear heart, no, it's not. It is not. Sean, I lied. I don't think all this is supposed to protect us. To keep us safe. I'm afraid it is supposed to … it is supposed to contain."

"Like, what? A disease? That doesn't make any sense."

"It doesn't, you're right, but … something very ugly. Scary. We're not allowed to leave the hospital. The staff! This means there's even less of a chance of you just, I don't know, making a run back to the apartment because you're missing a toothbrush or something. This is … bad is not even the right word. It's –"

"We read the letter in your apartment. We took the boys for a walk. It was … we were on our way out of town."

"That letter is old news now! Are you hearing me? They may not let you leave this hospital. My gosh, they may not let you leave this unit. And the patients? Kat? I'm so sorry."

A commotion outside the flimsy walls. One of the armed guards on the wing raises his voice. It wavers with panic.

"What is that?!"

Another voice, an orderly or nurse.

"Code white! Code white!"

Someone shouts. More follow.

An alarm begins to blare.

Emergency lights flash.

Sean and Julie exchange identical worried looks. The dread of what might await on the other side crawls up their spines. They pull back the curtain of the empty room in tandem, revealing a bizarre spectacle already in motion. Several patients are out of bed. They're gowns open as they pace in tight, interweaving circles outside the doorways of their makeshift rooms.

Sean notices their movements are identical. A pattern. He watches as both members of the hospital staff and armed guards begin to approach them apprehensively.

Julie takes his arms, pulling him away from the unfolding scene and toward where they left Kat. The young aid rushes out just as they arrive, throwing back the curtain to reveal Kat seizing in her bed!

Her monitors are going haywire!

The electroencephalogram is all over the place!

More frightened, panicked shouts and screams from elsewhere on the unit. Through the thin material, it is apparent that several more patients are wracked with identical, violent seizures in the beds surrounding Kat's.

Julie steps in to assist, but Sean is stuck watching. He stands frozen as everything devolves. His gaze switches back and forth, changing the channel between his view of his wife's bed and the odd drama playing out on the other side of the curtain.

Suddenly, the patients that have been walking in tight circles simply stop. Still. Statuesque.

From behind their eyes, beneath the skin of their fingers, from within, they begin to … glow? Their material bodies translucent as, emanating from them, a strange luminescent anomaly, a kind of faint Borealis gently pouring out of their very being and lifting into the air.

The alarms fall silent, and so does everything and everyone else for a moment. Like taking a deep breath before …

All kinds of telemetry and equipment begin to sound and alarm erratically. Everything made of metal gently rattling; anything weighing less than a couple of pounds now somehow lifted gently from the ground or whatever surface it now becomes untethered from.

Nothing makes sense.

Staff members, guards, and bystanders are left confused and befuddled at best, horror-stricken at worst.

Sean is locked away somewhere in his mind as he struggles to process it all, unable to comprehend it. His eyes fall upon an orderly who slowly moves toward one of the nearby patients. That pail aura gently swirls about them.

Sean has no context, no words, no rules, or no ability to describe or understand what happens next. The orderly steps into the wake of the patient's weird, cascading glow. It moves around him, over him, through him. He's entangled in the emanating light for a moment; then, he stops moving.

The orderly's spine jerks, standing straight as if pulled by a cable attached to his skull. He's lifted just off the ground. The toes of his Crocs drag the linoleum floor.

Sean can see that the orderly is trying to catch his breath, but something is suffocating him. The absolute terror fills the man's eyes as he looks at the patient, who otherwise seems oblivious.

The orderly gasps for one last breath as if attempting to scream, but the sound of his terror never arrives.

In an instant, Sean watches as the orderly is turned inside out, unraveling on an atomic level. A kind of quantum evaporation. He bears witness to it all, simultaneously stunning and maddening.

SIX

Dissociated. Sights and sounds are overwhelming. Too loud. Too bright. Too close. Stifling. Time seems to hang between the orderly's last moments and whatever should come next, but Sean's mind can't quite get there. Log jammed with anxiety and shock.

His perception and senses are slowed, time thickened.

Somewhere someone might be calling his name.

"Sean …"

Is that Kat? Is his wife calling out to him?

"Sean!"

Or Julie? She was just here.

"Sean, we need to move!"

He barely notices as Julie pushes past him.

One of the containment wing's armed guards loses his composure. He draws his sidearm, yelling at the patient responsible for the, well, Sean doesn't know what to call it.

The guard's voice is lost in the confusion and chaos of panicked people, sounding alarms and a thousand other indications that things are going to hell very quickly.

Another nurse brushes by Sean, and he is jolted back toward reality. His senses return just in time to witness those same tendrils of light slowly reaching out from the patient again, now inching toward the armed guard. Without hesitation, he fires his weapon! Two rounds strike the patient in the chest, and they collapse.

The guard watches as life leaves the human being that was just so abruptly executed. That light, though, still reaches out from the still body. Reason abandons him. Without any further provocation, he turns, aiming and firing at the other patients without provocation, signs of weirdness or not.

He fires once, twice, another shot. Two more lives are taken.

Sean watches as the barrel of the gun in the hands of this unhinged man swings toward where Sean stands in the doorway of Kat's room. He's already stood by as three people have been indiscriminately killed.

The guard's mouth hangs open, eyes crazed, finger on the trigger. From out of nowhere, he is tackled by another guard. The gun goes off one last time.

Outside the building, perhaps from the roof overhead, another transformer explodes. The building is rocked.

What remains of the emergency lighting threatens to go out. There's intermittent flashing. On and off. On and off. Then, off for longer than usual before mercifully stabilizing.

Julie pushes back past Sean piloting a wheelchair. Her voice finally cuts through the mayhem. "You need to help me right now!"

The three of them exit the employee elevator onto a darkened corridor. Julie pushes Kat in the wheelchair. She's unconscious and still again.

It's quiet, but they're hesitant. The trio hustle past a break room and turn a corner.

"Down here," Julie says. "Past laundry."

The wheels of the chair squeak on the tile floor as they pass laundry services and a large industrial kitchen. It all seems deserted.

Julie nods. "Get the door."

Sean hits the door with his back and holds it open. Down another hall, and they're at the loading docks. Between two corrugated steel doors is a single point of entry/exit. It reads CAUTION. ALARM WILL SOUND.

Sean eyeballs it. "Maybe we'll get lucky?"

"One can be too lucky," Julie says. There's trepidation in her voice. "Do it."

The heavy door groans open onto the loading docks. Above their head from hidden speakers, a klaxon blares! They don't waste any time, heading down a ramp, past dumpsters, and out into the street.

Despite being well past sundown, the sky overhead is alive. Not just with colors cascading through the atmosphere but with the sound of helicopters, distant emergency vehicles, and the diverse cacophony of panicking humanity.

"Where are we going, Julie?"

"My van. Something told me not to park in the structure today."

Red and blue lights of a nearby police car.

"How far?"

She swings the wheelchair in front of him, letting go of the handles and digging into her scrubs. "Keep pushing. Right behind you."

A block or so from the hospital. Most of the action seems to be back the way they came. Julie hits her key fob, and the lights on her minivan illuminate their surroundings.

After adjusting an armrest and tossing stuff aside, they lay Kat in the van's middle row, elevating her head on an old jacket covered in dog hair. Julie digs in her scrub pockets.

"Here," she says. "Pretty sure this is a felony. Don't tell anybody. Ha."

Sean fumbles as she shoves a handful of pill pottles between his fingers.

Her voice is low with hurry and fear but also resolved. "Big pills for pain or other discomforts. Little pills are ... well, relaxation. More than two, and you're headed toward sedation. Sleep. Like, shoot for one, but no more than three at a time. Like, five hours a part. You'll have to judge what's best. Oh, these too."

In his palm, he finds the keys to her van.

"What? I can't –"

"Go, Sean," she demands. "Get her out of here. Find somewhere quiet. Away. Away from the police. Guns. Away from people."

The reality of her statement doesn't have time to fully hit because they realize they are not alone. One of the armed guards from the hospital stares at them from across the street.

He starts to make his way toward them but makes every effort to show that his weapon is tightly holstered and raises his hands up in an unthreatening display.

"I'm just trying to get home."

He moves by them, giving them a wide berth. "If you're heading out of town, you will have trouble on the main roads. Roadblocks everywhere. They're looking for anyone who's … like her."

He starts to head off, continuing up the street away from them and the hospital, but stops, turning. "

There's a service road that runs along the Dandridge. River clean-up. Dam maintenance. I used to fish there. Gates probably locked, but … if it wasn't, you could take that to state road 36. Back roads until you hit the highway. Good luck."

Sean and Julie stand watching as he disappears into the night and whatever awaits him. Julie turns back to Kat, looking down at her friend. She catches Sean's gaze.

"What about you?" He asks.

"I'll head home. Somehow. Done here. 'Sides, the boys are probably missing me something fierce. Who knows the state of my couch by now with all these helicopters and commotion about."

"Thank you."

She wraps her arms around him before going back to Kat. The young woman is out cold, eyes twitching behind their lids. Julie puts her hand on her rising belly.

Sean straps himself into the driver's seat, looking back over his shoulder as Julie speaks.

"Get somewhere quiet."

"Then what?"

"Who can know? Go with God."

She slides the side door shut and jogs back the way they came without another word or the slightest look in their direction.

It's better for everyone this way.

Making his way through town, Sean's body is electric with apprehension. Every house, every business, every building dark, snuffed out by a blanket of darkness. The minivan cruising down city roads with dead streetlamps is a moving target for anyone curious enough, law enforcement or not.

He eyeballs his mirrors and surveils his surroundings constantly.

At the next turn, Sean douses the van's headlights at the stop sign.

On instinct, he reaches for the turn signal. Instead, he stops, noticing not only that his hands are shaking uncontrollably but that there's another vehicle stopped at the next intersection down the street, its high beams a warning.

With the lights off, Sean slowly turns the minivan and heads away from their glow. He parks along the road. Turning off the engine and laying his seat back, he hides and waits. And waits.

No one passes. Not the sweep of headlights. Not the terror of an erupting lightbar.

When Sean sits up, there are no other vehicles on the road.

He takes a deep, long breath and cranks the car.

After making it a few miles in the dark as safely as possible, he spots it: the service entrance. Sean stops at the steel bar that runs the width of the gravel road. He risks turning on the headlights just long enough to see a single padlock and a length of chain keeping the bar from swinging on its big hinges.

The road on either side is too narrow or too rocky, not to mention a sporadic sprinkling of pine that the minivan could never maneuver through. There's one way.

He reverses the van into the road, braces himself, says a quick apology to Julie, and hits the gas. The collision costs him a headlight and a buckled bumper, but the van makes it through otherwise in one piece. In the seat behind him, despite the starts and stops, bumps and bounces, Kat never rouses.

Sean drives for as long as he can keep his eyes open. He only stops when he finds a vacant state rest stop near an old fairground.

After tucking the minivan beside a small, brick maintenance building, his body finally succumbs to his ebbing adrenaline. Sean collapses into a fitful sleep in the van's reclined driver's seat and dreams.

*Lapping waters along a shallow shoreline
kissing the sand with the setting sun.*

*The horizon stretches towards the infinite
depths above and beneath.*

SUNFLOWER

SEVEN

Kat wakes to find her husband watching over her. The light is all kinds of wrong for the time of day. Soft and warm like it should be, but, as always now, very off. Or maybe this is just what waking up is like.

She takes it all in. Unsure. Confused as things take form.

"Just, just … hey. You ok?"

It's Sean. His face and voice swim into focus.

"How are you feeling?" he asks.

"Bad. Like a college Sunday morning."

"Gross. Here."

He reaches behind the seat and retrieves a bottled water.

"Go slow."

He fishes for something else without looking. Eventually, his hands discover the treasure, and he retrieves it, opening a pack of peanut butter crackers. He hands Kat a few.

"Not much room in here if you can't keep it down. Try not to. Sorry, all the chocolate was gone."

"I think … we were at the hospital? Julie was –"

"This is her van. She's … here have a little more."

She takes a sip, still collecting herself.

"We're at a rest stop off the highway. Well, kind of behind it. I didn't want to chance it, but it's worked out. So far."

"I don't understand. What about the man … there was a man in the light with me? Maybe I was dreaming?"

She sits up abruptly, frightened and frightening him.

"The baby!? Is she …"

They look at each other for a moment trying to read each other's expressions.

"They told you?" she asks.

He smiles at her.

"You had a seizure, but the doctor told me there is nothing to worry about. Nothing. Let's focus on you, OK? Besides, I'm sure she'll tell you once you have some food. We are fine. All of us. We will be fine. I promise. I'll catch you up when we're back on the road."

"We're at a rest stop?" She tries to look through the van's windows. "Can I maybe use the bathroom then? Except you look like I'm harboring an escaped mental patient."

Her joke falls flat, given what he's seen.

"I think you're beautiful."

"I think my breath stinks."

"Like peanut butter."

He tries for a kiss, but she fights him off.

"Let me get some gum or something first."

"Fine," he lies, stealing a quick peck in the vicinity of her left nostril and upper lip.

They step out into the morning and realize nothing will likely ever be the same. The sky is bruised, for lack of a better word or any metaphor that makes sense. More and more snakelike waves of aurorae cut across the atmosphere in the morning light.

Sean hands Kat the jacket from the back of the van to shrug over her hospital gown (which hangs out of the bottom). Then, taking her by the hand, he takes the time to examine the contusion on her own arm. It is larger. Looks … different.

He doesn't bring attention to it as they walk together toward the rest stop. Kat manages another cracker on the way.

Luckily, the place seems deserted. So does the highway on the other side of the median. Right outside the bathroom doors, they pass a vending machine. The front glass has been shattered. Sure enough, it has been picked nearly clean. Sean gives Kat a guilty "when in Rome" kind of shrug.

Like everywhere else, there is no power. Sean opens the door for Kat. She steps in, hesitant.

"I'll put my foot in the door and stand here. Do what you've got to do."

The morning seems devoid of normal morning noises. No traffic.

No birds. No wind. Nothing. Then, the sudden splash of urine in the bowl.

Sean notices something across the way, a rack of maps and pamphlets for tourists passing through. Over his shoulder, he asks, "Can you manage in the dark for a second?

Rifling through the pamphlets, he sees a few that catch his eye. He selects them, folding them and placing them in his pocket. He begins to turn, but another gets his attention: a sprawling view of isolated and rustic cabins high in the mountains north of them.

He picks it up and opens it.

Come enjoy the beauty of the season!

Open October through April, the Winter Cabins at Pineview!

A plan, a real possibility, begins to form in his mind when, behind him, the vending machine sparks to life! Some remaining snacks and chunks of glass fall to the ground as the cogs in the old machine whir and churn.

His mind can't process what is happening at first, then ...

Fast, Sean shoves the door to the bathroom all the way open. Crumpled on the floor, Kat's eyes roll violently back and forth in their sockets. The florescent bulb above her is pulsing faintly, rattling in its ballasts.

He stoops to hold her. Her eyes cease their frantic dance only to bang open when they touch. The universe is caught in the depths of her pupils. Stars and planets and entire galaxies swirl in specks.

The bulb above them explodes, raining slivers of glass down on them. Sean winces as he arches his body up and over to shield her.

Sean struggles to carry her limp body to the minivan. Kat is still trembling as he lays her on the hard ground outside the van's sliding passenger door. He violently yanks it open on its track.

Reaching between the front seats into the console, he fishes for the pill bottles Julie gave him. Fumbling with the bottles, he tries to keep her pinned under his weight.

Straddling her on the ground doesn't feel right with the baby, but he doesn't know what else to do. Flustered, he gets one of the bottles uncapped, but it slips from his hands. Pills fall, scattering.

Nerves winning.

Unsure.

Scared.

This is unexpected.

Unreal.

Exasperated, he drops the paraphernalia in disgust with himself for failing double. Failing to help Kat now and failing to protect her in the first place. Chest heaving, Sean looks down at his wife ... and she's herself.

Terrified, but herself. Terrified of herself?

Of her husband?

Of whatever it is that is happening to her?

To them?

Sean watches as hot tears run from the corners of her eyes into her hair, but she doesn't make a sound. She doesn't have to. He slides off her, confused and ashamed.

In the dirt beside the van, they scoot away from each other, unsure. Wiping away dirt and tears with the sleeve of her borrowed jacket, Kat finds a pill hidden in her hair. Pinched in her fingers, she looks at it. Looks at him.

He watches her, the look of shame and the burden that contorts her face.

"I'm sorry," she says.

He can't help but hear the voice of a stranger.

"Stop," she says. "Don't look at me like —"

"Me too," Sean tells her. "I'm sorry."

EIGHT

In the console, a plastic straw bounces rhythmically inside an empty, oversized Styrofoam cup. It tick-tick-ticks to the beat of the open road. Otherwise, nothing.

What passes by outside now is mainly rural, two-lane blacktop. Trees and forgotten crops. Houses sprinkled here and there. Signs of family and farm life that was but have moved on.

Kat shifts against the door in her seat. Sean watches from the corner of his eye as she pulls a piece of the shattered lightbulb from her hair. A chill lingers over the drive.

In this tight space, they are as far apart as two people can possibly be. To add insult to injury, the gas gauge lights up ominously on the dash, approaching empty.

For the moment, they both pretend it's nothing, that there's nothing to speak of, as the wheels spin under them, carrying them further from the known.

The gas gauge mocks them; that damned little jerry can glowing orange on the dash, accompanied for the first time by a sarcastic little chime. *Ding!*

It's enough to shake them both from their own drifting thoughts and bring them back to the world and the rest of the worries they'd rather choose to go on ignoring.

As luck, fate, or coincidence would have it as the van continues to blaze a lonely trail through the dead center of what appears to be the middle of nowhere.

Just up ahead on the left stands a squat little cinder block garage.

As the draw near, the pumps out front look like they haven't been used since the first oil crisis, but sure enough, there's a warped piece of plywood propped against one with *YES GAS!* spray-painted in dayglow pink.

Worth a shot.

The sound of tires on gravel and nothing else as the van pulls into the small lot, rolling to a stop. Sean instinctively drops the van into reverse, not very hopeful. They wait.

A storm door fitted oddly into the side of the peculiar building opens. An old, industrious-looking redneck comes out, motioning for them to pull around and into the garage.

Alien, as it all may seem, Sean does as he's directed.

As the van clears the garage bay door, the wiry old man cranks it shut behind them and, without looking in their direction, reenters the building through another door.

Sean starts to say something to Kat – she might even want him to – but instead, he just gets out.

Watching him through the windshield from where she reclines, Kat feels the cold *thunk* of the lock by her ear as he leaves her again.

Before heading through the door and inside the building the geezer just disappeared into, Sean looks back. He doesn't know if it's anger or sadness hidden under the confused hurt twisting Kat's face. A profound sense of failure washes over him as he turns, entering.

Sean winces as he steps inside what passes for a customer service area. Some smell, pungent, lingers in the air: gasoline.

The dust-blown tumbleweed of a man greets Sean with a smile from behind a counter. He's got a few teeth more than most Jack-o-lanterns and long hair tied back in a ponytail. One strap of his overalls is unbuttoned; a tattered old *Nascar* t-shirt probably purchased back when Earnhardt was king clings to his bony frame underneath.

"Afternoon to ya! Gotta say I wasn't expectin' nobody much today. Well, not nobody 'cept the Lord coming on the clouds judging by the looks of that bedeviled sky. Name's Earl. Ya'll get in an accident?"

"Fender bender," Sean lies. "Sign said gas?"

"Gas? Got gas, yuh."

The old man nods to a collection of gas jugs, milk jugs, and other containers. "Not too many wheels on the highways and byways, I'll tell ya that. What with the, uh, government and all. Heard they're stopping just about anybody they spot. Turning 'em around, sending 'em home. Or, well …

"I can sort you out. Sure nuff", Earl says. "Been a lonely day. I'm ramblin'. What's the world like this fine day?"

Sean rummages a nearby end cap full of snacks, taking note of a sparse assortment of crackers, jerkies, and nuts.

"It's a, it's kind of … it's what you'd expect." Then, as if the gears click into place, Sean shifts, stooping. He scans the goods and grabs a couple of chocolate bars, an apology.

"No chance you got any ice cream stashed?" Sean asks.

"Ha! I'm no miracle worker, unfortunately. A couple of these coolers up here with plain ole ice in 'em. Got some sodas. Bottled water. Even a few beers, cans mainly."

Sean tosses his small haul on the counter and moves to the side where the gentleman has three coolers lined. He throws them all open but only grabs a couple of water.

"Strange," Earl says, looking over everything on the counter. "I mean, this all starting with the whales?"

"Whales?"

"Them whales? Beaching themselves? Come on now, all over the internet. Of course, the news didn't make a fuss about it, too busy going on about the President. But … they was talking something about their, uh, internal navigation? You gonna want a bag?"

Without time for an answer, he begins bagging Sean's things before continuing his story.

"I never heard of anything like it, but whatever it is, was being affected by, uh, what was it? 'Increased solar activity.' Mmhmm. I remember 'cause someone was clever enough to call it a solar tantrum. Some kind of fit, yeah. Believe that? Solar tantrum."

At that, Sean, nearly involuntarily, looks over his shoulder to the door that leads back to the garage.

"Take it with a grain of salt," Earl continues. "Media being what it is nowadays."

"Power was bad enough, I guess," Sean commiserates.

"Oh, don't get me started, telling us to sit –."

"In the dark."

Damn right, son. And for what?"

"They never really said."

"Never said! That's right. Never said. Little secret: I got an old radio back there. I let the generator run a little. Careful. Real careful. But I been listening to the chatter on the Beartracker – police scanner, ya know – just here and there, what there is."

"Oh yeah? What's the chatter?"

"Gotta tell ya, not no chatter like I ever wanted to hear. Something about the magnetic fields in space. The Earth and the Sun. I don't understand too much, but ... chatter like I never.

"There's even tale of folks wearing tinfoil. Tinfoil! Tinfoil hats? Remember when they was 'sposed to mean you was the crazy one! Now, you know, what a world. Whatever. Mumbo jumbo, but also: police. Lots of military. Martial law. Huh, speak of the devil, and he shall appeareth."

Sean follows the old codger's gaze out the hazy windows and catches a State Police cruiser passing by.

"How much gas for you, son?"

Sean breaks his gaze, fumbling for his wallet. He should have thought it through. He only has a handful of bills, less than thirty dollars total.

The old man takes notice.

"How far are Pineview Cabins from here?"

"Pineview? Pineview. That's up near Tulok? You can get there on, what, maybe three-quarters tank? Hafta stop somewhere along the way if you wanna make it back, I suppose. Unless you want to tote a jug to go?"

Earl laughs. Sean checks over his shoulder again. His eyes widen as he turns, his capacity for humor abandoning him as the police cruiser pulls up outside the garage.

"Pineview? Say, ain't that a winter place?" Earl asks.

Sean has half-zoned out. The state trooper is slowly exiting their vehicle. Both men at the counter watch as the trooper eyeballs Earl's makeshift sign with curiosity.

"I ... uh," Sean stammers. "I just remembered ... I'll um ... need to check something."

He shoves his wallet back into his pocket, spilling a few precious bills without notice before scooting out the service door and into the garage just as the policeman enters the opposite entrance.

There's no mistaking Kat's frustration as Sean re-enters the garage, but her expression shifts as it catches up to the look in his own eyes. She watches as he hurries to the garage door, yanking the chain beside it. It slides up with a clatter.

There may only be a couple inches of clearance between the door and the car's roof, but Sean has the driver's side door open and is behind the wheel, turning the key.

"Police," is all he says.

The van is in reverse and moving when the customer service area door opens.

Earl gives them a quizzical look as they back out in a hurry. He shrugs it off. As the door shuts, he makes his way to the officer hoisting a five-gallon jug of gasoline onto the counter, just another motorist in need.

The minivan catches a tire, squealing pathetically as they pull out, leaving the garage behind them posthaste. Sean has a death grip on the steering wheel. His eyes are wide. They keep getting lost in the rearview, along with his focus. That cruiser will be right behind them any minute now with its lights flashing.

The road ahead of them is an afterthought. Paranoid. Sean runs his hand through his hair and lets it fall beside him. Kat's hand finds it like a stranger across the console. Sean flinches, jerking away from her.

She's wounded. Sean knows.

The van pulls over along another stretch of farmland a few miles from the garage. Sean gets out, leaving the driver's side door open. Kat sits, watching him as he begins walking up the side of the road as the van's door alarm chimes.

A good ten or fifteen paces away, Sean doesn't turn to face her when he hears the passenger side door shut behind him. He stops.

"We're married about a month," he says. "That's when I had the dream. This dream that I've had versions of ever since. Off and on. Over and over."

Kat approaches, listening.

"We're … somewhere? Somewhere," he keeps on. "There's … water. A lake? Pond? I can see the sunrise reflected in it. Maybe the sunset? I don't know. But, you're there, I know it, but … I can't find you. Wherever we are, wherever you are, I can't find you. I'm looking.

I can tell that I'm looking; I'm looking everywhere. Worried. Scared to death.

"The night you told me you were pregnant, I had the dream. The same ... the same one. Again. And, and I can't find you. I'm calling out. I'm yelling ... I'm always ...

"I've had the same dream over and over, and it's never the same, but it's never different."

As he shares his story, Kat slowly makes her way to him. Standing just a few feet apart, it's the closest they've been – the closest they've felt – since the morning.

"I always find you," he says, turning toward her. "I find you in the water, the sunlight playing off. You're not moving. I always find you, but I can never save you. I lose you over and over and over."

She takes a step toward him. So close. As close as breath.

"We were there. You. Me. Together," Kat starts, a little more than a whisper. "Whether it's the end or the beginning ... we were there."

He turns around to face her.

"The next time you dream, when you dream that dream, try to dream it differently," she tells him. "But if you ever stop looking for me, if you ever stop looking for me, no matter what you find...."

By the side of the road, she reaches for his embrace.

"Promise you won't stop looking for me."

"I always find you," Sean says, taking her in his arms. "I'll always find you."

Above them and around them, the sky is dazzling.

Dancing.

Dangerous.

NINE

Kat moans in her sleep, reclining in the passenger seat. Sean looks away from the road, glancing over to check on her. She seems peaceful enough, but for the last couple of miles, every couple of the whines that have escaped her dreams have been followed by a rather violent series of tremors.

The first took Sean by quite a surprise. Her flailing hands. The snap of her head to one side. Most disconcerting were the windshield wipers. They had come to life all on their own. The engine and dashboard gauges fluttered.

Eyes on her, she moves a little, adjusting, but seems well enough, considering.

Sean turns back to the road in front of him just as a large utility bucket truck pulls out in front of him! He slams on the brakes. This is the first vehicle he's seen on the road for some time. Sean pulls the van into the passing lane and lets his foot off the gas as the big truck goes down the road, seemingly unaware.

The gas gauge remains a constant reminder on the dash: they are approaching empty fast.

Sean watches as the utility truck puts on his blinker about a half mile further down the road. Curious.

He slows as the truck in front of him turns into a small diner snugged up against some woods. A hole-in-the-wall joint like everywhere else they've passed for the last hour, but there's a large barbeque pit out front. Smoke bellows from its bowels. A decent line of hungry-looking folks buzz about chatting and smiling, waiting to get some chow.

Sean begins to accelerate by when Kat moans, and a tremor radiates from her and through the van. The whole thing shudders. The engine threatens to die. He grabs the wheel and starts to pull to the side of the road as all the lights pulse and the gauges flicker on their own.

About the same time the van rolls to a stop, everything normalizes; everything behaves as it should, including the steady, ominous glow of a nearly empty tank telling him over and over it's just about the end of the road.

Sean tries the engine. It cranks without trouble. Flicking the turn signal, he scans his mirrors before pulling back onto the road.

In the rearview, the diner and the promise of warm food.

And people. Strangers.

His stomach rumbles as if on cue. Digging in the console for what remains of their stash yields very little. Finally, he looks up again, eyes reflected back at him before catching the waft of smoke from the barbeque trailing in the air.

"No," he says to himself, putting the van in drive.

Something else gets his attention, though. Just across the road, at the far end of the diner's gravel lot, and just at the tree line, a weathered shed. Parked beside it is a riding lawn mower. On the ground next to it are two red gas jugs.

On the dash, the gas light mocks him.

On the seat beside him, the pamphlet for the cabins beckons him.

The van pulls onto the blacktop as Sean turns the wheel hard, heading back toward the diner. Cautiously, Sean allows the van to creep through the gravel parking lot. He appears inconspicuous as he rolls past a small crowd spilling out onto the diner's covered porch, moving around the back of the building. The minivan sticks out, as the primary clientele drive pickups or motorbikes.

Kat sleeps, curled against the door, using her borrowed jacket as a pillow. He watches her, the rise and fall of her chest. Her body is still, with no twitches or tremors. With no safer options, Sean leaves her again, locking the door behind him again.

He heads toward the back of the property, making his way to the mower. Giving the first jug a shake, he is dismayed to find it empty. He's reaching for the second when the backdoor of the diner opens on loud springs. Sean sees an apron-clad short order cook pop out of the bag carrying a bag full of garbage.

There's nowhere to hide. The cook spots him.

"Hey, buddy! What are you up to?"

Sean thinks fast and feigns fumbling with his zipper.

"I'm so sorry, I, uh …."

"We got bathrooms inside. The world's going to all hell, don't mean we can't pretend to be civilized. Come on."

The cook leads Sean in through the noisy door. They cut through the back of the diner, past the quiet kitchen, to where h shows Sean to a small bathroom.

Paying Customers Only.

The cook gives him a wink and a smile. "We'll make an exception if you promise not to water the weeds."

When he enters, a couple of tea lights are burning on the sink and the back of the toilet. Sean is relieved to relieve himself. He flushes, and the toilet makes a weird gurgling, chugging noise. The sink doesn't work either. The pump must be electric. A bottle of hand sanitizer beckons him.

In the mirror, Sean catches a glimpse of himself. He looks tired. Aged. It could be the light, but his appearance makes the last twelve hours seem more like twelve years.

The bathroom door shuts behind him; Sean looks back down the hall, where the friendly cook led him through the building.

The plan is to get back to the gas.

Back to the van.

Back to Kat.

Voices are coming from the opposite direction, though. Even fits of laughter. Signs of real life. Of normal.

A line cook moves past him, coming from around the corner, with a big platter of raw beef. Hamburger. Steaks. Roasts. Sean follows him toward the sound of people and the smell of something delicious.

At the front of the diner, folks are milling about. They sit at tables lit by candles as, outside, the sun is in its final moments of glory before heading to bed for the night. Through the window, the sky is still broken. Ominous. Threatening. No one seems to be paying it any mind, though. Plates of barbeque, brisket, sloppy burgers, and chips are being shared. There's even a guitarist that looks like he's carved from the same wood as the stool he's perched precariously upon while a motley handful of crooners sing country classics.

The short-order cook finds Sean taking it all in.

"Not bad, huh?"

"It smells great. Looks … divine."

"We make do, don't we? That's the American way. Do you want something? Better get in line. Once the sun is out of here, so are we."

"The curfew?"

"Eh, ain't too worried about that. 'Sides, we got quite a few good ole boy types here. The law'll look sideways with a smile and roll on by. They know we ain't starting no trouble. But, naw, we just don't wanna burn through all our propane just yet. So? You eating?"

Sean's stomach churns. Suddenly, he's never been so hungry.

"Couple of burgers or something for the road?" he asks.

"Sure thing," the cook says. "Find a seat, and I'll have somebody get it to you."

"How much do I owe you?"

"Didn't you hear? It's all going to go bad. On the house. Of course, there's a couple tip jars." He winks.

Sure enough, there are several mason jars around the diner. Most of them overflowing with bills. Big bills.

Sean saddles up to the diner's bar. There's something both comforting and threatening about the way the vinyl seats groan under his weight; the feel of plasticware and napkins on the linoleum counter. Like, play-acting when the world is on fire around you.

He can't help but eavesdrop on the conversation exchanged beside him. Sean listens in as an older gentleman with bushy, untamed eyebrows hidden just under the brim of a leather brush hat gets into with his younger, but still several years Sean's senior, stool mate.

The second man is lean. Something about him seems hardened, tense. Of course, it could just be his five o'clock shadow, which gives him a very intense profile from Sean's point of view. For a moment, their eyes meet, and there's ice in them. Sean looks away, intimidated; his hearing still inclined, though.

"There ain't no way," the elder goes on. "If that was really happening, don't you think it'd be all over by now? You're sayin' –"

"You're telling me you trust the news, that you trust the government, to be honest, Hank?"

Now the eyebrows belong to a name, at least.

"Course not, but others? You think you'd hear from somebody you know if what you're talking about is really –"

The hard man cuts him off with a raise of his plastic knife. He cuts a piece off his hamburger steak, running it through a thick pool of steak sauce before shoving it into his mouth, speared at the end of the knife. "We'll see."

"We will." Hank nods. "You're right; we will. I hope your insider information, premonitions, and predictions are more grounded in reality than some of your other nonsense."

"What are you on about?"

"Me? I've been knowing you since your daddy took you into the woods to hunt your first buck. Then, I had to listen to his conspiracies and politics. Now, I've inherited yours. God rest his soul."

"Lucky to have been accompanied on this earthly journey by two such fine fellas, you ask me."

"The Dahl men," Hanks says, poking at the man beside him. "Daddy and junior. No finer. No meaner."

"I ain't no junior, and a temper keeps you alive."

"Not if you keep eating like that," the older of the two old men adds, taking a bite from his own greasy burger.

With his focus lingering on the edges of their conversation, Sean fails to notice the Styrofoam plate on the counter before the aroma hijacks his brain.

"Oh, man," Sean moans.

"Whoa! You must be some kind of hungry," says the man with a stern face and cold eyes. There's almost a smile behind them deep in there. Somewhere.

"Been a ... a long day. Night. I ... we've been on the road."

"Yeah? Where from?"

"Headed to –"

"No," the man asks, any traces of levity leaving. "Where from?"

"Uh, just South aways. Couple hours."

"I heard some rather interesting stories coming from down that way. Uh-huh. And, did you, you say we?"

"My wife."

"Where is she?"

"She is, just, she's outside. Getting some air. Stretching her legs. Pregnant. Yeah, she's pregnant."

"Well, congratulations," Hank says, leaning onto the counter.

The man he now thinks of simple as Dahl measures Sean.

"Why don't you go get her," he says. "The missus can take my seat. Me and this old fella were just about to wrap things up."

"Who are you calling old?" Hank retorts.

"Well," Dahl says, turning to his friend. I'm going on 'bout old as dirt, so that's gotta make you, what?"

"Hmm. Old as the stars above," Hank replies. "I suppose."

Sean watches as Dahl stabs the last of his food, chewing slowly and deliberately. There's spit when he talks next. But he doesn't seem to mind.

"The stars. Yeah. The shining stars above. They're something else nowadays. Where ya'll are coming from, couple hours South you say, what seems to be the talk about all that?"

"I haven't, really," Sean starts. "Actually, I, uh …" He waves down the short order cook. "Can I get something to cover this?"

He turns back to the two men, one far more interested than the other.

"I should probably go check on her."

"Sure, sure. Before you do," the hard-looking man says. "I heard – besides the police and the military, besides the roadblocks and the power; an overall threat to our freedoms – that people are getting sick. Sick folks, maybe even dangerous folks."

"Leave that boy alone and let him go get his lady," Hanks says. "He just wants to get something to eat, not one of your earfuls."

"Here you go," says the short-order cook. He's brought a big roll of aluminum foil, stretching it over the Styrofoam.

"That plates starting to look like some of them folks coming out from down your way. All covered up with tin foil and baking sheets. Damn, I think you may want to protect yourself with something more substantial."

"Like lead?" Hanks asks. "Doctor's office has those aprons."

"Lead? If that's the case, I got plenty," Dahl says.

Sean sees the large revolver holstered at his waist for the first time as the strikingly tall man stands, tucking his shirt in and plucking his cowboy hat from the counter.

"Stay safe out there, young man."

Hank watches as Dahl takes a couple paces toward the door. He spins a key ring around his finger. A toothpick now perches on his lips.

"Never said where you were headed, fella."

"I, uh, actually."

Sean pulls the folded pamphlet for the cabins from his pocket.

"Am I headed the right way?"

"Yeah, buddy. Just keep up this way a bit. You'll hit 16. Keep west. Not too far off, nah."

"That's good news. We're pretty low on gas."

"I'd like to say I could help you there, but sorry."

That's when the men notice it's gotten quiet. The guitarist has stopped playing. The crooners have ceased crooning. The general level of murmuring and babble has died down.

Sean follows the silence to where everyone else's attention already seems to be drawn. At the front door stands Kat.

She's standing there in nothing but her hospital gown, looking exactly the way he'd hoped she wouldn't be.

People are reasonably freaked out, and that's before the lights – the lights that aren't even on; the fixtures with no power - start to hum. Patrons watch as some begin to flicker. As bulbs buzz and rattle in their fixtures, expressions of wonder and curiosity are replaced with a shared nervousness as a subtle electric rhythm begins coursing through them.

When they reach their limit, blinding, they begin to burst, shatter, and spray shards of glass and filament. Whatever spell has bewitched them seems to dissipate. Folks are scrambling to get out of the way and figure out what to do next.

Sean tries to get to Kat, but she might as well be a million miles away. He watches as a waitress wearing her miles around her eyes, a genuine expression of concern in them, attempts to reach Kat. He cannot hear what she says, but it makes no difference. There's no one there to talk to.

Sean's stomach turns. He feels sick as he watches a thick thread of blood ribbons from Kat's nose and down her chin.

The eyes of the stranger wearing his wife's face begin to glow.

The young lady stops, backpedaling away.

Dumbfounded, Sean can only watch as the woman he loves begins to move, spinning in those same weird, tight circles. A pattern. As if she is dancing with the light that slowly comes from her and everywhere else at once. Dull, nearly imperceptible, but intensifying.

At first, it is all just like at the hospital. Electromagnetic anomalies. Anything metal becomes incrementally untethered from gravity. Floating. Hovering.

The aurora flowers from her. Blooms. Interweaving. Pulsing. Resonating within her, the slow dance of her body moves to some unheard tune.

Then, it's everywhere!

This permeating otherness manifests in spectrums of translucent color moving around and through everything. What began as quiet of awe has transformed into a din of fear, quickly becoming screams of agony.

The waitress, beset with worries of her own and a story we'll never know, the kind woman who only wanted to help, goes to her knees and several others close by. They press their hands against their ears, crying out against whatever they're experiencing.

Sean is surprised and terrified to see that somehow Hank has made his way to her. The kindly old man reaches out for her gently. He keeps his hands raised. He only wants to help.

Meeting her gaze, or the gaze of whatever lies behind her eyes now, Hank falls to the floor clutching at his chest.

For a moment, Sean stands as frozen as everyone else. Just another bystander, wholly dissociated. Nothing more than a witness.

He watches as Dahl, the hard-looking man with coldness in his eyes, closes the distance between himself and the ailing man, crying out.

"Hank! Somebody?! God! He's having … his pacemaker!"

Sean pushes through the cloud of noise, people, light, sound, and time that has enveloped them all to reach the table.

"What's wrong with her, dammit?!" Dahl screams. He turns to Sean. "What'd she do to him?!"

Around them, more people are grabbing at their heads. They are trying to dig out whatever has gotten in there. Some of them watch, rapt as the weird light flowing from nowhere and everywhere entwines them. A few more try to staunch nosebleeds.

Sean sees Hank's key ring dropped on the floor by the man's motionless hand. Vibrating. Rising just a hair above the floor.

"We've gotta do something."

Sean meets Dahl's gaze. There is madness there. His teeth grit. His stone face is set.

"Gotta stop it. Gotta stop her!"

Now, the keys are hovering about knee-high. Sean looks to Dahl, to the keys, and to his wife. He grabs the keyring, but Dahl swipes at his wrist and knocks them back to the floor, where their weird rhythmic pre-flight dance is reset.

Dahl looks confused until he follows Sean's gaze to where Kat stands. Then, if it's even possible, his face hardens more, and the older man gives Sean a flat-out deadly look. On the floor, Hank begins convulsing, stealing his attention.

Sean takes the opportunity to scoop the keys from the ground. Then, hooking Kat around the waist, He pulls her toward the exit.

TEN

A seething mob crashes through the diner's doors and clambers onto the porch. Their eyes narrowed to slits, mouths twisted into sneers, all bared teeth and rage like a horde of villagers storming after a monster.

Perhaps they are. After all, whatever else Kat's presence triggered, it also seems to have flipped a switch inside the patrons who weren't entirely overcome by it.

Dahl leads the pack. He is screaming, frothing, working them into a frenzy.

Sean can't make the man's threats out over the pound of his own heart. His feet scramble for purchase in the unpaved parking lot as he drags Kay backward, his arms hooked under her own, her bare feet trailing in the gravel.

Pressing every button on the stolen key fob repeatedly, he tries to get a bearing on where the vehicle the keys belong to might be parked.

Luckily, a nearby truck – a big diesel – chirps a welcome as Sean presses the button again in desperation.

Kat is returning to herself as they reach the truck. As Sean opens the passenger door, she greets him with more confusion than recognition. Despite that, she's able to climb inside with his help. The mob is nearly on them now. Sean scrambles through the passenger side door, up and over Kat, locking to the door as it slams shut just as the big truck is swarmed.

Through the glass, he comes face-to-face with Dahl.

Humanity slowly seeps back into those hard eyes, but it is evident that whatever animal Kat may have unleashed lives caged behind them all the time. He tugs on the door, trying to get in.

As Sean slides behind the wheel, another irate man makes it to the driver's side door and responds in like fashion.

The rest of the swarm stands in front of the truck, a human roadblock. Some even place their hands, many smeared with their own blood, on the hood as if they can hold it in place.

"Get out of the truck!" Dahl demands.

Sean fumbles with the gear shift, which prompts Dahl to quickly take a step back, teeth barred and fueled with rage. Before Sean can get the vehicle into gear, Dahl's boot connects with the door. He takes another step back as Sean pulls Kat toward him, shielding her, and kicks the truck again!

Dahl stalks, his mind bathed in an unrelenting, primal fury. Whatever voice of reason typically withholds permission to allow him to go to this place has been silenced. He finds a piece of nearby debris, a chunk of broken concrete, and uses it to punch through the passenger side window! Sean and Kat wince against the violence and the glass. Dahl tries to reach in, despite the broken, jagged edges. Sean finally forces the truck into gear. They are moving!

The swarm in front of the truck promptly parts. Dahl manages one last aimless swipe with his boot at them, his arm now bleeding from the broken glass.

Sean shoves the stick forward, and they're kicking up gravel on the way out of the parking lot.

In the rearview, Sean watches as one of the fellows checks on Dahl's bleeding arm. The belligerent man pushes the others away. He barks orders, and the rest scatter.

The stolen diesel barrels down the road. In the sky overhead, the aurora seems to race lazily after it like a river of iridescence carving a mirrored path through the ionosphere.

In the cab of the truck, none of those elaborate details matter.

As Sean guns the engine, the wind threatens to send more broken glass whipping through the interior. Kat instinctively covers her face against the possible onslaught, snuggling into his side for protection.

He looks at her. There are pieces of glass glittering in her hair. Rivulets of blood from tiny cuts trickle down the hands covering her eyes. She winces as a piece of the tempered glass detaches from the spiderweb of the fractured pane and hits the rear window behind her head. Sean sees nothing of the power spilling through her at the diner, only raw vulnerability.

The diesel slows as Sean pulls it to the side of the highway.

"Here," he says, shrugging off his shirt.

He leans over to Kat, watching for the glass as he opens the passenger door.

He uses his shirt to block the window, closing the hem in the door.

"Not perfect, I know."

They look at each other, him in his undershirt, a day and a half's worth of stubble now prominent on his face, and her in a hospital gown wrapped in an old coat; both flecked with glass and looking so very over it.

He smiles at her.

"Thank you," she says.

"I hope it holds. At least keeps most of the glass from …."

He mimics something that resembles being pecked by birds.

"I meant the smile," she says. "I like it when you look at me like that. Not the other way. Not like back there."

She delicately uses the jacket sleeve to knock glass into the floorboard. Then, she slides away, staring out the windshield.

"I don't know how much longer we have," she tells him.

"What are you talking about?"

"I know you're scared, and that's alright. It's alright, but I'm not scared. I promise. It's ok."

"What are you saying?" he asks. "What are you trying to say?"

"You'll see it, I promise. It's everywhere. Everything. The beauty."

"I don't –"

"When I was little, like seven or eight," Kat says. "I went to see my grandmother. I didn't know it, but she was in hospice. She told me, one of the last things she told me, she said, 'It only goes one way, darling, so make sure you find someone to make the trip worthwhile.'"

What strikes him the most is the self-awareness she speaks with

There's no reservation.

They don't have time to finish the conversation.

Sean sees them in the rearview mirror before she has a chance to finish. A few miles back, vehicles approach way too fast. He shoves the diesel in drive and kicks up dust as the heavy tires find purchase.

A motorcycle reaches him first. Big and heavy, the cycle's engine roars as its rider pulls alongside and motions for him to pull over.

Sean looks away, his food on the truck's accelerator. No way is he stopping.

Ignoring his problems has seldom made them go away. This is no different. The rider perched on the squat, beefy motorcycle swerves at him, attempting to intimidate him.

Sean doesn't think. He's had enough of it all. Everything. He is fed up, weary, and now angry. Taking his foot off the gas, Sean cuts the wheel towards the motorcycle to send a warning.

The rider backs off, but Sean's antics are costly.

The trucks have caught up.

One is right on his bumper.

The other approaches on the other side, riding the shoulder. Even with the passenger side, he drifts closer to Sean, forcing them into the oncoming lane.

Kat leans into Sean as he grips the wheel with both hands.

All they can hear is the growling of its engine and the flapping of Sean's shirt wedged in the doorframe as he accelerates while trying to keep control of the big truck.

They watch in horror as the shirt is gripped from the other side and torn away. Pieces of glass fall into the cabin and fly about. In the gaping whole staring back from the other truck, one hand on the wheel and the other bloody fist clenched around the shirt before releasing it to the wind is Dahl.

"Pull over!" he shouts. "Now!"

Sean watches as the man pulls his arm back into the pursuing truck's cabin to steady the vehicle. He turns his attention back to what lies ahead, not acknowledging the threat. Set. Determined.

Unwise.

"Sean!" Kat screams.

A gunshot erupts in the space between the vehicles! Sean looks over. The trucks are even again. Dahl brandishes the revolver.

"Next one's going in the tire," he threatens. "The one after that …."

He trails off, looking down the length of that big gun barrel.

Sean notices the truck behind them slowing, not so close now. He grabs Kat tight, slams the brakes, and yanks the wheel to the right. The maneuver works. Whoever is following in the other pickup, a little cautious already, brakes hard, creating space. Sean corrects his steering and is now behind Dahl's truck. He gives the gas pedal everything, butt raising from the seat as he applies force, willing it to be enough for what he attempts next.

He collides with the other truck, pushing into it while cranking the steering wheel.

Another gunshot rings out in frustration, but the pursuing truck that has become the pursued jolts as it is forced hard toward the shoulder.

Dahl's thinking is blurred with adrenaline, rage, and vengeance, he overcorrects, and the big truck spins, nearly going up on two wheels, and then settles hard on the middle of the road facing the opposite direct.

Although pursuing cautiously at a distance, this tactic costs the motorcyclist, who comes careening toward the stalled truck. The rider steers to evade it but loses control and spills the bike on the asphalt.

Sean weaves by them both, accelerating and hoping this means their followers might reconsider whether they are any longer worth the trouble.

Sean keeps on the gas while adjusting the rearview mirror. Kat sits up, looking out the rear window. Behind them, no one gives chase.

Yet.

They both stop holding their breath, releasing some of the tension that has gripped them for the last several minutes.

"They won't stop," Sean says flatly. "Maybe we slowed them down, but we've got to get off the road."

Beside him, Kat falls against the broken window.

"Hey!" Sean yells. "Hey, hey!"

He leans with one hand on the wheel and takes her by the shoulder, pulling her back into his side.

There's no fighting it. Kat is heading out again, leaving him for mystery. She looks up at him, the slightest smile before her eyes close.

Her body hiccups.

Her head snaps violently.

Sean tries to hold onto her, pressing her shaking body tight against his own. He can feel her trembling, but also something else. The truck is trembling too. On the dash, the check engine light illuminates. He can feel the power draining from under his foot as he stomps the accelerator.

"No," he says as a lone pair of headlights appear in the rearview mirror. "No, no, no."

He continues to push the diesel to its limit, which is working against them now. Behind it, a solitary pickup catches up. Dahl.

No warning shots. No attempts at conversation over wind and through panes of shattered glass. Dahl barrels down on them and swipes at them with his vehicle.

His first attempt is unsuccessful. Sean attempts to get out of the way on his next try, but something under the hood gives up the ghost, and smoke starts belching from the engine compartment. It's hard to see.

Dahl swipes at them again with his own vehicle and snags their bumper!

Panic and smoke fill the cabin as Sean tries to keep on the road. His tires hit the shoulder, then the truck leaves the pavement. He hits the brakes as they go off the road, careening down a shallow, wooded embankment.

He holds onto Kat as they bounce and shimmy. One of the tires fails, a loud blowout. Sean knows how this will end, so he braces them the best he can. The truck's front end wraps around a tree, deploying the airbags. It is not a pleasant stop.

The stolen diesel has disappeared into the woods at the bottom of the ridge. The beam of one remaining head lamp illuminates the surrounding branches at an odd angle. Taillights are barely visible through the brush and foliage that blink out. The motor gurgles its last few breaths.

In the dark, Dahl's headlights approach the wreck.

Sean fights with the airbag. It is covered in blood from a cut at his hairline. He winces. His wrist might be injured, too, sprained at least. Maybe broken. The cabin is smokey and full of glass.

He asks Kat, "Are you here?"

"I'm …," she replies.

"You ok?"

"… I don't know," Kat answers.

"Gotta get out."

"Help me."

Sean fights the driver's door open as Kat struggles to slide through the glass and stubborn, impotent airbag. She winces, a surprised pained sound escaping her lips. Sean watches as she pulls a long piece of glass from her leg. Blood trickles from the cut, but nothing too severe.

"Come here," he says, helping her to her feet.

They scan the direction from where they came. Thirty or forty feet up the embankment, Dahl's headlights cut through the dark.

"Can you walk?" he asks her.

"Do I have to?"

"I think so."

He stoops and pulls his own shoes off. Kat seems out of it again and doesn't fight him as he puts his shoes on her feet.

"We've got to be quiet."

When he pulls the second set of laces taught, they hear someone stalking their way down the hill toward them. He guides her as quickly as he can into the darkness.

They're still within earshot of the crash but well hidden in the shadows of a moonless night when Sean stops. He grimaces, sinking to the ground so he can massage his foot.

Looking back the way they came, they listen. The sound of their pursuer. He's found the truck. The engine is put out of its misery with a final gurgle. The lights are extinguished. Suddenly, the woods are a lot quieter and even darker. They flinch as Dahl screams with rage! A quick flare of light followed by a hollow boom as Dahl fires his gun once, twice, a third time! Sean recoils, the last shot cutting through the trees only ten or fifteen feet away from them.

"You saw it!" Dahl yells. "You saw what she did! What she is! I hope you can hear me! Both of you! You better never leave these woods! You better die out here!"

They can hear him kick and hit the truck repeatedly in the dark. A destructive outburst.

Sean looks at her to see her reaction, but her expression is unreadable. Distant, even as she clutches her belly.

"Kat?"

Nothing. Losing her again.

He waits until Dahl's footsteps fade, climbing back up the hill before coaxing her deeper into the woods.

ELEVEN

It is too dark, and branches and vegetation are too thick to make out much more than the sound of a creek nearby. No way to get their bearings. Sean and Kat rest. Allowing the trunks of the trees to carry the burden of their fatigue is the only thing keeping them from giving themselves over to fatigue.

For a moment, just the sound of their breathing.

The shallow running water nearby.

The subtle movements of the forest around them.

"You're bleeding," Kat says. Her voice should be comforting in the stillness around them, but there's something unusual in how the words come out as if she's never used them. As if she speaks with someone else's mouth.

"I'll be fine," Sean says as chills crawl over his body. He tries to ignore the goosebumps the rise on the back of his neck. He checks his wet socks. There's a hole in one heel, and three toes on the other foot have made their own escape. Both feet are moist and raw.

"Your head," says that not-quite-Kat voice again.

"I said I'll be fine."

Sean pulls back, catching the traces of exhaustion and exasperation that lace his own voice. He wills himself to be gentle and reaches out for her.

"How is your leg?" he asks.

Kat grazes the outside of her thigh with her hand and shows him. It's patchy with sticky, drying blood. It could be worse.

She closes her eyes and leans further into the embrace of the tree.

Then, without warning, her body slides down, making a slow, controlled descent to the forest floor. Her legs spread out before her,

her torso propped against the trunk, head lulling to one side.

Sean knows she's out again. He's growing uncomfortable with how routine this all is becoming. He crouches, getting down to her level.

Her chest rises and falls peacefully.

He brushes her hair out of her face.

"We can't be out here all night," he says, mainly to himself. "Alright then."

Standing, Sean tries to grab her gingerly under her arms. A pained moan escapes her throat as he attempts to stand with her. He leans her back against the tree, trying to position her to at least allow for a façade of comfortability.

"I guess we're staying put then."

He fidgets with her, shrugging off his coat and wrapping it around her. He pulls leaves around her legs for warmth and to pad her landing if she falls over in her sleep.

Sean removes a branch that threatens to stab her from under her knee. Then, reaching for another stick that can't do too much damage but might leave an excellent scratch if allowed, his hand grazes her thigh, and it comes away dirty with fresh blood.

He quickly checks the site where the glass from the broken window cuts her. Messy and gross, but almost dry, a scab already forming.

No ...

Sean slides his hand up the inside of her thigh. It comes away slick and bloodied, his fingers nearly black with it in the absence of moonlight.

He's carrying her through the woods. Sticks and rocks tear at his feet; his shoes still tied tight on her feet, hanging lifeless at the end of her limp legs.

She moans in his arms as he follows the creek where the land begins to rise.

The water flows through a wide concrete culvert at the bottom of an embankment. Closer, Sean can make a path snaking up the hill toward a guardrail a few meters up. The tell-tale sign of a road.

Sean ducks into the culvert, fitting in the tunnel with Kat in his arms. The splash of his sodden socked feet barely echoes back from the void at the other end of the underpass.

In the dark, away from the entrance, he lowers Kat, leaning her against the cold concrete wall.

"I'm going to get help," he reassures her, even though the only one listening is himself to the sound of his own words reverberating back at him. "This is the last time. I promise. I'm not leaving you again."

He bundles the jacket under her to keep her out of the water as much as possible.

A single kiss on her forehead.

"I promise."

Knowing he'll be unable to pull himself away if he waits any longer, Sean doesn't even consider looking back. He has no choice but to leave his wife in the dark, cold, and wet. Eyes on the guardrail and his chances cast on whatever lies beyond, he starts up the hill.

Sean scrambles up to a narrow, single-lane gravel access road. He listens for the sounds of vehicles. There, distant and down the road to his left. From the sound of it, he thinks it can't be more than a mile from the main road. That settles it.

Keeping to the side of the road, cautious, he jogs in that direction, but it isn't long before real life catches up. He's tired and hungry. His mind is in a million places at once. And overhead, that bastard sky.

His estimate off, Sean stops to catch his breath again. His socks are worthless, so he yanks them from his tender feet.

Walking is better than standing still and getting nowhere, so he holds onto what little hope he dares to dream and the image of Kat's smiling face like a glowing lock screen in his mind.

The gravel meets the blacktop, and something catches Sean's eye: the bumper of a sedan.

He creeps forward.

The car is parked under broad branches of an old-growth tree overhanging a lonely turnout just off the narrow back road. It's the kind of place young lovers might escape, experimenting with their bodies for the first time.

Cautiously, Sean approaches. Low, he makes his way to the driver's side window. There doesn't seem to be any movement inside the vehicle. Sean raises his head slowly to look inside through the back window. People! They don't move, though. Never again.

As Sean steps around the vehicle, blood and gore splattered on the driver's side window, he hesitates before opening the door.

The dome light illuminates the scenario. The car's occupant's story is straightforward. The man in the passenger seat slumps against his door, a gunshot to the temple. The driver must have them put the gun in his mouth and pulled the trigger.

Sean shuts the door. Queasy. He dry heaves.

Taking a moment to compose and ready himself, holding his shirt over his mouth, he braces and opens the door again.

The dome light again. Also, a faint dinging. The keys are still dangling from the ignition. Respectful of the dead man's body and wary of the blood, Sean closes his eyes and leans carefully over the driver to feel for them.

His fingers graze the keys just as the subtle presence of his own body causes the corpse behind the wheel to slump just so. Sean quickly retracts himself from the vehicle, on the verge of hyperventilating.

He takes a few quick, gentle laps around the turnout, wincing as his feet collide with sharp stones and someone's discarded beer bottle cap, all to psych himself up.

Averting his eyes, Sean is quick this time. The gore is hidden in the blur of his periphery. He yanks the keys free from the ignition, and the faint chime stops, and that's when he sees it. The gun. It must have fallen to the floorboard.

Sean sets the keys on the dashboard.

The gravity of what the weapon has already accomplished is evident in how delicately Sean reaches for it. Feeling the weight of it in his hand, he examines the gun. It is much lighter and smaller than one might expect for so much carnage.

His precautions betray him for a moment. Sean looks past the gun in his hands, noticing something new. The two dead men in the front seats of the sedan parked under a kissing tree are both holding hands.

Possibly lovers with a death grip on each other in their last moments together.

Even more moving, when he takes the time to really look, to really see, the man in the passenger has the same tell-tale discoloration spreading up his arm as Kat.

It's vining up his neck, veining out from his temples.

Whatever happened here was the end of this couple's story, the very same story of what might happen – *is* happening – to them.

Sean drops the gun and falls with a clunk back into the floorboard.

His body collapses against the opened driver's side door, but his mind is elsewhere. Great heaving sobs takeover his body. His breath hitches in his chest. It's all coming out, the grief and anger and fear.

Retching, crying, he stands and retrieves the keys from the dash.

With tears streaming, breath caught in his chest, anguished in his throat, Sean shuts the car door. He uses the keys to lock it, to lock the men inside with each other. Then, before he can second guess himself, he throws them as far into the woods as he can manage and collapses.

As he takes the first step onto the shoulder of the main road, Sean looks terrible. Unkempt. Shoeless. The victim of both a vehicular and an emotional wreck.

A peek over his shoulder, back the way he came, before willing his bare feet to follow the white line. It is enough to just keep putting one foot in front of the other.

The road is empty. So is Sean. All he can do is keep walking on legs that want to fail and a mind so tired of thinking. Then he hears it, a deep rumble. Looking up from his dragging feet, Sean sees approaching headlights. Something big. Something that sounds powerful. Ominous.

Apprehension grips him. Do those headlights seem familiar? Is the sound of that engine recognizable? It is hard to tell.

For the first time, the possibility that Dahl and the others may still be out there haunting the highways and scouring the night for them creeps into his mind. Add that to the anxiety tally.

Sean squints against the dark and the oncoming lights, both working against his vision. It is definitely a truck. A big truck. Is it *that* truck?

It's over. Here he is: about to be beaten or shot or, hell, runover in the middle of the night, left to bleed out on the side of some country road, while Kat and the baby …

In a moment of panic-laden decision-making, Sean turns his back on the approaching truck and shuffles down the side of the highway toward a thicket a couple yards away. Clumsy with nerves and adrenaline, his poor feet trip him up. He falls hard onto the shoulder before scampering into the tree line, the notion that the driver has seen him nags unavoidably.

Perhaps they're doomed, either way, discovered by roving sociopaths or neglecting the help of a random driver simply on their way home.

The truck slows.

Sean catches his breath and grimaces at the scrapes on his palms and knees. He watches as taillights erupt with a flare of red His eyes and body flood with terror as the driver pulls a slow U-turn in the middle of the road!

There's nowhere else to go, no plan B, so Sean tries to make himself as small as possible among the skinny trees and brush.

Headlights pointing down the wrong side of the road, a spotlight erupts from the driver's side as the vehicle's wheels crunch to a halt. The door creaks on old hinges; all his fears are confirmed as someone adjusts the light directly on him.

He can't see them, hidden behind the blinding spotlight.

His ragged breathing and steady pulse are the soundtrack of time crawling on broken limbs.

"I have to be upfront with you," says a strong female voice from opposite the spotlight. "I have a shotgun trained on those woods. Out of politeness, I'm just letting you know. It's getting late. I'm old, but age hasn't taken my good sense yet. Please don't mistake this as an opportunity to act uncouth. Let me see ya."

Sean rises slowly into the light, raising his hands even higher.

"Hello there," says the voice. "By way of transparency, I also have a rather hungry mutt goes by Raphael stretched out on this bench seat beside me. He doesn't mind strangers but knows where his food comes from. So we would both prefer you to be friendly. Are you friendly?"

"Yes," Sean manages. "I am. I'm friendly."

"Being the trusting passerby that I am, how can you help me understand that my acting as a Good Samaritan, though as guarded at the moment as I may be, will be met with courtesy, friend?"

"You're the one who's armed."

"So you say. Tell you what: stay in this beam and keep the conversation civil, and I'll put my gun down. Deal?"

He nods.

"What are you doing out here in the middle of nowhere? Middle of the night? You alone?"

"Yes, ma'am. I mean, no. My wife, she's waiting on me. I went to look for a ride. We were … in an accident. She's pregnant."

"Uh-huh. How come, if you're out here looking for a ride, for help, how come you turned tail when you caught sight of me?"

"The accident … there was … it wasn't an accident. A man, his friend, I don't know what to tell you or how to explain it. We were run off the road by this fella. My wife is bleeding. The baby … she's a mile or so back the way you were headed. Off a side road or something."

Nothing from the voice for a second. Sean just stares into that bright spotlight.

"How pregnant? How far along?"

There's kindness in the voice that wasn't present moments before.

"Shy of twenty-five, twenty-six weeks?"

"Boy? Girl?"

"Little a, a little girl. I didn't want to know. I wasn't supposed to find out. She wanted to tell me. Yeah, we're having a little girl."

Silence.

The spotlight goes dark with an audible pop in the dark. Sean's eyes adjust slowly as he hears the door shut with some trouble. Footsteps on the tarmac in the dark. Someone coming toward him.

The barrel of a shotgun appears first. It is angled slightly lower than Sean's midriff and is carried by a striking woman in the sunset of middle age. She is compact but lean, a tangle of gray hair spilling from under a ratty bucket hat. Glasses. Her eyes are bright with life.

"What do I call you?" she asks.

"I'm Sean."

"Name's O. Miss O. Let's get your wife, Sean."

She motions with the gun. Sean walks timidly toward her classic pickup. "Jump up in the back, if you don't mind."

As she opens the door, Sean sees a small Pekingese sleeping stretched out on the bench seat. He couldn't hurt anyone but himself.

TWELVE

Sean rides in the truck bed as it bounces down the gravel service road. Miss O slows and gives him a look out the back window as they pass the parked sedan in the turnout. He just shakes his head and motions for her to keep driving.

Just before arriving at where he climbed from the culvert, Sean smacks the truck's roof. Miss O slows and pulls to the side. Sean hops out and hastily climbs the guardrail.

O flips on the spotlight and scans, following him with it as he scratches his way through the brush before disappearing down the hillside. She waits.

An uncomfortable amount of time passes before the young man appears in the ring of the spotlight again. O's heart breaks as she watches him struggling to carry an unconscious young lady up the shallow hill. Kat is soaked through in the thin hospital gown. O notices the intake bracelet still shackled on her wrist. Thin rivulets of blood trick down her legs. O shakes off the shock and climbs out of the old pickup.

"What's her name?" she asks, opening the passenger side door and snatching the blanket hiding the seat's torn leather upholstery from under the lazy dog.

"Kat," Sean says. He's winded. "Katherine, but she hates that."

Miss O helps Sean get her situated in the bed of the truck. He cradles his wife's head in his lap. O helps get the blanket tucked around her.

"Nice to meet you, Kat. Let's get you someplace else."

Sean falls in love with the beautiful old woman as he watches her climb behind the truck's wheel. The look on her wrinkled face in the rearview mirror tells him the same.

They're in this together, an instant family of strangers.

The spark of a lighter as a candle catches flame. Sean holds Kat in his arms as Miss O strips the bed clothes back.

"Get her in here," she instructs him before squeezing by to light another candle. "Get her out of that rag and cover her up. I'll be right back."

O shuts the door behind her as Sean carefully lays his wife on the bed. He de-gloves the wet gown from over his wife's head. The discoloration on Kat's arm has spread. It reaches its way up the musculature of her neck. The same ominous tendrils creeping up her arm radiate out from her belly, a horrifying pattern of concern.

The door opens behind him, and he covers her up.

O steps in, holding a gas lantern. She's got some old clothes and towels over one arm, a bowl of soapy water gripped in the other hand. It sloshes and spills a little, but neither pays the mess much attention.

"My husband was a vet. I don't even keep animals on the property anymore, 'sides from Raph. I have two kids and helped deliver more than a couple of foals. May I look?"

Sean nods. She does.

"Still bleeding, though it's light. Troubling, but it could be worse, I suppose. We'll keep an eye on her."

Kat groans and shifts in the bed.

"Let's start with something simple," O directs. "Got some water. Hope it's not too cold now. We need to get her - both of you - washed up."

She tosses the clothes on the foot of the bed.

"Not going to be much in the way of style, but we know what they say about begging and choosing. Get some towels under her. It could be a long night. I'll be down the hall warming up some more water."

She leaves them.

Sean dips his hand in the bowl. Then, ringing out the washcloth, he wipes the day's grime from Kat's face.

Sean opens the door to find Raphael staring up at him. The small dog's nails click and clack as he pads down the hall, leaving Sean to follow him toward the flicker of flame and the hiss of another lantern.

He leaves the door cracked behind him.

Miss O is fiddling with an old propane camp stove as Sean enters the kitchen. She gets a burner sparked and sets a pot on it to boil; beside it is a small tea kettle.

"There's a case of water by the fridge," she offers. "Bring a couple bottles and empty them in here. Take one for yourself."

Sean bends and pries a few bottles of water from their plastic binding.

"She seems ok," he says. He begins pouring. "Still seems to be in pain, but I'm not sure. Bleeding is …"

Sean nurses his own bottle. He takes sips like he's never fed himself before; his thoughts are all over the place. Maybe no place at all.

"Catch your breath," O tells him. "Have a seat. You look like you've run a marathon. Something to eat?"

"Doubtful."

"I'll throw on some soup once the water's boiling. That way, you'll both have something warm, if ya' like. But, you know, I would have never stopped tonight. Normally, I mean. It's silly, really. Even you sitting here now? Funny, kinda."

"Why did you turn around?"

"Could've been a bad idea, huh?"

"Might still be."

"No. No, I don't think so," Miss O says, taking a seat across the small table. "I was on my way home from church."

"They have church on Tuesday?"

"Right? Some folks would have church just about any day, some of 'em. With everything going on here lately, they have been keeping the doors open all day, every day. I'm not particularly fond of the whole thing. But my husband, well, he was the church person."

She looks into Sean's eyes long enough to know he is paying attention, willing to end the story there if need be. His eyes meet her own, and they seem amicable. Honestly, she's been lonely, and it feels good being here with someone. Hopefully, he feels the same.

"We'd get dressed up," O continues. "I'd sit in the pew beside him every week. Not because that's how I wanted to spend the morning, no. I did love watching him. I loved the sound of his voice as he sang those old songs. The way he smiled and just came alive. I hadn't stepped foot in a place like that since his funeral. That was his place, after all. It seemed almost rude to go without him."

The tea kettle whistles, and she sets about pouring and steeping. Finished, she rejoins Sean at the table, a small spoon in her mug. Steam drifts lazily.

"How long have you been married?" she asks.

"Two and a half years. Ish. Met in college, though. That was something like eight years back?"

"Met how?"

"It was my junior year, two weeks after my twenty-first birthday. There was this bar. Many people would go there for, like, beer and, trivia; karaoke. I've never been much of a drinker. Much of a singer. That night, a buddy of mine, Kyle, convinced me to leave my apartment and enjoy a belated and inebriated birthday.

"This girl I had kind of been crushing on buys me a beer, gives me a smile, puts a microphone in my hand. Then, I proceeded to bomb so hard, but I was committed. I got that beer down; someone handed me another. The next thing I know, it's my turn again. I get up there, and from the stage, I see her. That girl, my crush, is making out so very hard with a dude at the bar. No big deal. We barely knew each other, but …

"I start singing again. Sort of … *awful*. The next thing I know, there's this other crazy, drunk brunette with the biggest smile and this mischievous sparkle in her eyes on stage with me. She rescued me from embarrassing myself, as she has over and over.

"We spent so many nights there. Sometimes just snuggled up in a booth eating bar food and watching others make asses of themselves. So, yeah, that's the story. Almost ten years ago now. I mean, compared to you, I'm guessing that probably doesn't seem very long."

"Seems long enough to really know someone. To really see them. I am a little envious, though," O says with a wink.

Sean watches her look away for just a blink, sipping her tea and replaying memories she alone carries.

"I went to church tonight," she says, turning back to him. "I went because I was scared. I don't know a person who can't look at that sky up there and not be. I mean, a week ago, what? They tell us it's nothing. Solar flare? Then …"

"Then the power," Sean commiserates.

"Leaving us in the dark. Literally." Her face takes on a firmness. It isn't directed toward him or their conversation, just their situation in general. "No explanation. Maybe won't ever get one. And I was scared. I didn't need the prayer. The sermon. The people, let's be honest. Sometimes they're the worst part of the package. But, no, I just wanted to go somewhere I could see him."

"Did you?"

"No. No, Sean, he wasn't there. But, on the way home, you were. You asked why I stopped? You looked as scared as I was. Seemed like what he would do. What Peter would do."

She stands, touching Sean's shoulder to steady herself. Then, she begins transferring the hot water to a ceramic bowl at the counter.

"I'll put that soup on. You go, be with her. I'll be in shortly."

Sean slowly opens the door. Closing it behind him, he kneels at the bedside.

"I don't know where you are, where you've been. I know where I'd like you to be. Where I'd like us to be."

Without being fully aware of it, his fingers begin to trace the faint map of this calamity that crawls just under her skin.

"There's something I need to tell you, and you're not going to think it's very nice. You hate it when I fib, though. The day you told me ... the day we found out we were going to have our baby? I was, I was so mad. I was angry at myself. I was mad at you. I just ... I didn't want to lose ... what? Us, right? I didn't want to lose you and me.

"Is that really it, though? Or, am I ... am I scared someone else might need you? Scared to let you rescue someone else? To let someone else love you?

"I don't know, but right now, I'd give anything to be standing in the bathroom door watching you sit on the toilet in tears, reading that little strip. Because that's you and me. And she's you and me, and maybe she won't need you to rescue her ... because we'll have each other."

His fingers trail from her elbow, following that alien pattern towards her wrist.

"Where are you?" he asks again.

As he reaches for her hand, almost completely covered now in that faint veining and bruising, he hesitates, but her fingers unfold like a flower, welcoming.

"Right here," Kat says.

He looks up, and her eyes are opening too. Her gaze is weak and unfocused, but that's her looking back at him. It's her.

"Right here?" Sean asks.

"For now," Kat answers. "For now."

"Can't you stay? Will you?"

"You're still afraid."

"Not of you. No."

"We don't decide where it takes us."

He takes her hand in both his own.

"Kat, we don't even know what this is. You could be, I don't know, you could be hemorrhaging. Your brain, your mind –"

"I know what I see. I know who I am. I know who we are, and it's beautiful. So don't be afraid to let it find you."

He lets go of her hand now. His body is warm with anger he never wanted to feel. "So, what, I let you … go?"

"You're still afraid," she says again. "That's ok."

He's barely holding it all together.

"It's just not you, Kat! Have you felt … have you felt our little girl? What about her?"

She smiles weakly at him.

"I feel her all the time. Just like I feel you." She squeezes his hand, and the bulb in the lamp beside the bed flickers.

"All the time."

Down the hall, something clatters to the floor and breaks. Probably a soup bowl.

"It's ok to be scared," she tells him. "But don't stop looking. It's already here. You'll see."

Kat is gripped by a tremor in the bed. This time it is accompanied by every light in the house flashing on and off. On and off, with every convulsion.

"Hey, hey, hey! Right here, yeah? Right here. Stay here. With me? Please?!"

In the throes of her fit, Kat kicks the covers off one leg, and Sean sees the bedsheet covered in blood. Her back hitches, arching. She wails miserably. Miss O hurries into the room, shoeing a nosey Raphael back out. The door shuts in his tiny face.

O looks at Sean, neither of them sure what to think, say, or do. Then, over the next few terrible moments, Kat goes into spontaneous labor.

Time ceases to exist in the confines of that small bedroom, a purgatory of cries, tears, and anguish. It reeks of sweat and iron. Eventually, mercifully, it is over. Kat delivers.

O tells them both over and over how brave they've been. She tells Kat she did a good job, an excellent job.

As far as Sean can tell, Kat doesn't hear them. Her breath is shallow, pulse thready, and her mind elsewhere. Only now does a part of him, a deep and secret part, pray that she doesn't wake up.

The little baby girl she's born into the world doesn't cry.

She will never cry.

THIRTEEN

Above the house, the starless sky is alive with that heavenly aurora moving in waves rhythmically so far above. The farm might as well sit at the epicenter, in the eye of this swirling solar storm. If you ask the old house's occupants, they may very well report it does.

From where she looks out of the window, Miss O must admit it really is quite alluring. She catches her eye growing captive, drawn in despite the wreck of a human being that shares the bedroom with her and the poor young woman lying whose hand she holds even now.

Sean sits in the corner of the bedroom, knees drawn to his chest. Between hitched breaths, primal moans escape from a broken place deep within. His hands shake, teeth chatter. In his arms, he cradles their baby. A beautiful girl, lips blue and eyes forever closed. His entire being responds outwardly to the confused emptiness that grips him inside. Every time he thinks he can collect himself, the sight of her little, lifeless limbs ruins him anew; soul torn and heart broken, again and again. The spiral of a birth mark works its way up her tiny arm. A birthmark that is too eerily like the pattern snaking along his wife's body in the bed beside him, slowly overtaking the entirety of the woman he loves. The ineffable thing that is consuming her; that took their child. For a moment, he allows his grief to yield to anger. He doesn't understand any of this. It makes no sense. How could she ask him to understand, to see what she sees? Everything in him feels betrayed, wounded, left for …

Miss O can sense the shift from where she's been sitting silently at the window. As Sean stands, she takes the opportunity to step into his pain.

"Let me take her. Just for a little while," she says.

She examines his face, the face of a man fighting to keep the final pieces of himself, his world, from slipping through his fingers and into nothingness. Something else, though. Something has changed; his perspective shifted, broken, as he looks at his wife's face.

"She's been through so much," O says. "You both have. You all have."

Another wave of grief threatens to hijack his emotions and his body as he gets to his feet, but Sean holds the pieces together a bit longer.

He hands this kind stranger his daughter wrapped in an old blanket. His expression is warmed by the way she cradles the infant to her body.

"You're going to be OK," she tells him.

She leaves him with Kat.

Kat.

She's out again. Maybe for a long time.

Maybe for the last time.

Sean gently traces the bruise on her arms. He follows its course from her wrist up her shoulder, then down to her wedding band. Using the blanket, Sean wipes the blood from Kat's nose. He moves the damp hair away from her face, the face of the girl with the mischievous eyes and most genuine smile now sunken. Her skin appears thin and translucent, with tiny veins and capillaries cutting their way under the surface. The thing inside her, all around her, above her hollowing her out. For a moment, he allows his hand to find her belly. It lingers there long enough for the sobs to well up inside of him once more. It feels like what's left of him falls to pieces on the floor by the bedside.

There is no beauty here.

Sean closes the door and makes his way down the hallway on legs that don't feel like his own. He finds O in the study. It's a small room overflowing with books spilling off the walls and collected in stacks on the floor. Easels bearing canvases lined like soldiers along the wall opposite the windows. Some of the handmade canvases are painted. Some were deserted mid-project. Others remain blank, untouched. Some of them are pretty good. Others are great. One catches his eye, a brilliant close-up of a sunflower. It's all browns, oranges, and the most exciting shades of yellow. A fascinating perspective, disc florets, and the edges of several beautiful outer rays. The detail is painstaking. Hours of skillful, careful touch. A fire burns in the fireplace, embracing the room with warmth.

Miss O stands in the corner, gently rocking the child. She doesn't shift her attention from the child as he studies the painting but acknowledges him.

"They were Peter's," she says. "Been here like this since the last time he was in this room. I'm still not quite ready to pack them up or throw them out if that tells you anything."

Sean moves to her, holding out his arms. She places the baby into them.

"I'd love to know her name," O asks.

Sean doesn't offer an answer. O shows him an antique basket where she's placed a pretty little blanket and a sprig of dried flowers inside.

"I found this," she tells him. "To rest."

Sean's appreciation is subtle. Subdued by grief and denial. He looks at their stillborn child, taking her in for a moment more before covering her tiny face with the blanket with finality.

"Your husband seemed like a good man," he says. "Talented. An artist. A healer, too."

"He was all that," O replies, those memories playing behind her eyes. "We always say those kinds of things, but I meant it then and mean it now. Loved his work. Loved animals and people, too, most of the time. Loved his books. Lord, as you can see. Loved his paints, maybe the mess more than the finished product. Wanted to create something to just see it come to life. None of the baggage of sentimentality, but now, ironically, I cling to them."

"She's suffering, isn't she? There's no way she's not. Just a matter of time now."

O looks him in the eyes and speaks when he'll meet her own.

"The man lying beside me in bed at the end of it? Some days, I felt like that man was not my husband. Like he'd left already by then. Punctual even in the end. Part of me left too. Parts. A little here, a little there, because once he was gone … I couldn't come back. Not all of me. Not all the way."

She stops to poke at the fire before moving to where he stands, looking at the painting.

"For a long time, I hated how much of a stranger I'd become to myself, but I found pieces of us along the way. Like a puzzle with him and me on the missing box top, just going on memory and feel."

The fire burns.

"He's probably more of me now than he was before," she tells him.

Sean examines an unfinished painting. There's even still a paint brush on the easel, dried permanently to the tray.

"They say art is never finished," he says. "Only abandoned. Never completed, just forgotten. Left behind. Do you think the same can be said about relationships? To give ourselves, all of us, so hard and so fast to it, and then … you just wake up one day, never suspecting things to change, but they do."

She watches with a twinge of agony as he snaps the brush from where the last human fingers to touch it placed it. Sean doesn't notice what he's done; the impact of his gesture is lost.

"I'm sure … I'm sure your husband, I'm sure he dealt with many animals that were too injured to be tended to. Aid would've been … maybe even selfish, to prolong the inevitable just because you can't say goodbye?"

They look at each other, both understanding what is being considered between them.

"I reckon he was in a lot of discomfort toward the end, too?"

The weight of the situation now sits heavy. O looks at Sean, the infant swaddled in his arms little more than a prop now, along with the neglected paint brush in his hand. He's barely even there, she can tell, just moving limbs and features while the rest of him is locked somewhere behind a wall of feelings no one would choose to be trapped by.

"I flushed it all not long after his funeral," she tells him. "Least what they gave him."

For a moment, his eyes. The tears damned behind them reveal the truth. Perhaps the woman lying bedridden down the hall's suffering is nothing compared to the shattered soul standing in front of her.

"Tell you what, though," she offers. "Let's lay her with her mama, then we step out to the barn."

Sean helps shoulder open one of the barn's large, wooden doors. It creaks open arthritically. Miss O carries a flashlight that reveals further evidence this place has sat undisturbed by anything more significant than a healthy rat making her home in old hay for some time.

In another life, the smell and sounds of animals would have permeated the space. Instead, years have removed all the energy and color, save for a few signs of what was. They find their way to a door with a frosted glass window. The ghost of a name spelled in vinyl letters clings where a razor blade couldn't find purchase. Miss O pauses with her hand on the doorknob.

"This is where Peter did consultations and little things. Stitches. Sometimes emergency stuff, for neighbors mostly."

She slowly enters, stepping into the dusty clinic. Sean follows reverently.

"Friend's new Saint Bernard swallowed a paint roller and ended up here," she tells him. "I remember that. Dog the size of a pony. Had to put her out. Hold this."

O hands him the flashlight, the beam following around a desk. She grips the back of a plush chair. It gives a little under the pressure as she gently knocks the dust off it.

"Been years," she says. "Used to find Peter out here late. Wasn't much of a drinker."

Sean watches her lean forward and opens a drawer on the desk. Miss O sets a worn pack of playing cards on the tabletop. Her hand wipes away more dust. She opens it, pauses respectfully, and then spills the cards onto the table.

"I'd find him out here," she continues, a smile in her voice. "Playing solitaire of all things. Way past dark, but he'd be out flipping over cards. Decompressing, I guess."

She sits in the chair and begins laying the cards out as she speaks. "Not every day was a bad day," she says, flipping them over a few at a time. "Most were good. Hard sometimes, but good."

She pulls a key from the same drawer and puts it on the table with the cards.

"Cabinet on the wall," O directs Sean. "Open it up. If there's anything in there, bring it here. Be quick with that light."

He does as he's told. Inside the cabinet are a few different bottles and some veterinarian paraphernalia. None of the words or items mean anything to Sean. He takes a little less than an arm full back to the table and shines the light on it. Even in the dark, O has played a few moves, stacks of cards bigger than they just were.

She picks through the pile of pharmaceuticals reading labels. Then, slowly, she holds one vial out to Sean.

"This. It would … this one would work. Pentobarbital."

They look at each other in the dust and darkness, contemplating what the next hour of their life will entail in different ways.

Sean takes the vial from her and pockets it.

O nods. There's a resolve to her gesture but still a hint of reticence.

"You'll need a syringe. Needles and the like are in the drawers over there, if there's anything left."

She has him hold the flashlight so that she can play another card before nodding permission for him to take it and retrieve what he needs from a cabinet across the room.

"What you said about art? About relationships? It struck me back there," she tells Sean's backside as he rummages. "It struck me because it's not true. We don't abandon anything, and everything we ever lose comes back 'round again. In one form, one face, or the other. Nothing is ever wasted."

"It doesn't feel that way," Sean says, rummaging.

"I know, dear. I know, but we can't let the cloud of our suffering add to the suffering of our world, even if our world is just a handful of folks we hold the closest for the briefest of times."

"I don't see it, O," he says through tears. "I don't see what she sees; how she sees. I couldn't before all this, and I can't now."

Sean's eyes land on a sealed syringe. He reaches for it with trembling hands.

He doesn't hear Miss O get up from the chair and her hand on his shoulder is almost too much to bear with his electric nerves.

"Some nights, I'd find him out here after a long day or a bad day, and I could see it in his eyes. Flipping cards and trying to work something out. I'd say … I'd say, 'You look a little lost.' He'd smile, and every time – *every* time – he'd say, 'Do you know the way home?' Sometimes I'd sit with him while he finished his game. Sometimes I'd help him clean up, turn off the lights, and walk over for supper. Sometimes, we'd sit. We'd sit right here and talk, or not."

O reaches for the syringe. Sean lets her take it.

"You look a little lost right now, but … she's been your bearing up until now, so, maybe if you let her, she can save you again; show you the way home?"

Sean's body quivers as he allows himself to be wrapped up in her arms.

In the slender trays of the metal cabinet, in the beam of a flashlight held in the quaking hands of a sobbing man, the few stray instruments that remain begin to rattle just so. An invisible pulse sends what can only be described as a shockwave through the barn, their bones, and their very beings. They both steady themselves and catch their breath, their hearts hiccupping and heads spinning as the receding wave causes misfires and palpitations throughout their bodies. Across the room, a lamp on Peter's desk blinks twice, then flickers to life before the bulb is overwhelmed by the power coursing through it and pops. The flashlight sputters in fits as Sean and O look at one another.

Sean wipes at his own face, but only O's nose is bleeding.

SUNFLOWER

FOURTEEN

Those lights in the sky, a dim window into an alien world. Sean steps out of the barn and is momentarily swept up in its madness, mystery, and magic. The cascading dance overhead defies knowledge, understanding, and reason, an ancient rhythm underlying existence.

The barn's tin roof threatens to peel off; the groan of the tarnished metal pulling old nails from worn trusses brings Sean back down to earth. That and the sound of sirens.

Miss O staggers out behind him, grabbing at his arm and pulling Sean toward the house while pointing his attention to the road. A quarter mile down her long driveway, a parade of pickups and police are turning off the main road at O's mailbox. They speed toward the homestead.

The flashing lightbars and the wails of police don't frighten Sean half as much as the vehicle leading this spectacle. Dahl.

"Get to it, boy," O says, yanking him along. "Not the time to drag your feet."

Her legs fail as another pulse radiates out from the house. The irony isn't lost on her. Sean grabs for O, steadying his friend even while his equilibrium is pummeled. They trudge together towards the very thing that threatens to overtake them.

Over their hunched shoulders, the convoy of pickup trucks and cop cars kicks up dust and debris, speeding in the same direction. Sean turns, watching with surprise as the approaching vehicles enter the current of the anomalous wake. It's like hitting an invisible barrier, slowing their speed; the procession momentarily stalled as their engines struggle against it.

It buys Sean and O some precious time. Inside the house, Sean puts his back to the door as O turns the deadbolt and slides a chain lock near the top.

"Some of your friends from earlier?"

Sean moves to the window, peeking out. "Why now, though?"

"Meanness is often motivation enough," O tells him. She reaches into her pockets and shoves the vial into his hand.

They look at each other. Close.

"I didn't get a syringe," he confesses. "I couldn't. I could, but I didn't. I can't."

She puts her arm around his neck, pulling his forehead to her own.

"I do wish things were different. I do."

She reaches up and grabs her keys from where they hang beside the door. "My truck. If we can … If I can keep 'em talking."

"I don't think they want to do much talking, O."

Outside, the vehicles' lights surround the house.

Another violent pulse.

They ride it out together, hands holding onto one another.

"I don't think we can outrun this," Sean tells her before handing back the keys. That's when someone knocks on the front door.

The house is surrounded. Headlights and law enforcement lightbars flicker, disrupted intermittently. Their engines and electronics stutter, parked in the middle of this weird, brewing, cosmic storm.

A tall man stands backlit by the blinking lights and the chaotic bulb of the porch light overhead. He knocks again.

Miss O greets him as the door opens, catching on the chain lock. She peers out at him, and the rest of the mob gathers in the night.

The man has his big fist raised, callused and strong, just about to knock again. Dried blood darkens his lip and oozes from his ears. He smiles at her. Blood in his teeth, the corners of his mouth flecked with it.

The man named Dahl smiles at her, but there is malice behind those eyes. It shakes her more than she'd wish to admit, but Raphael's brave presence in the crack at the door, snarling his tiny snarl, gives her the courage to stand her ground and do some growling of her own.

"Awful late for solicitors," she tells the crazed man.

"That's some guard dog," Dahl replies.

"He does his best."

The man watches O reach out of sight to the other side of the door, drawing her shotgun close.

"I figure I can make up for his slack."

The tension builds in the gap of the open door.

"You're fun, lady," Dahl says. "I wish I was in the mood to humor you. It's far too late for feigned pleasantries, however. You know why we're here, who we're here for. Not too many places in this neck of the woods sitting dead center of whatever the hell is goin' on out here and up there."

"If I say I don't know what you're talking about or who you're talking about?"

"Then my patience is going to run out real quick like. How'd you even end up in this?"

"We're all in this. Whatever this is. Look up. This is bigger than one young woman."

"So, you do know who we're looking for? If that's the case, why on this cursed earth are you putting on this feeble display?"

"First, it seemed like what Peter would do, " O says flatly. "But he ain't here now, and I am. And I want you to leave."

She racks the shotgun. On the porch, Dahl smiles through the crack in the door as she closes it in his face. Dahl looks over his shoulder, resolved and ready. He nods to those gathered behind him. On the other side, Miss O collects herself, adrenaline pumping. She brings the shotgun up, ready. Not ready enough, though.

Dahl's heavy boot kicks the door in! The wood frame buckles, and the chain lock is shorn off. The door catches Miss O in the shoulder as it flies open on its hinges. She's spun around, falling to the hardwood floor. Her shotgun lands a few feet away on the rug. Raphael slips in at her side, yapping. Furious but impotent. Dahl steps over the threshold. A few rough-looking brutes follow.

O is surprised that, judging at least by their attire, more than one of them seems to be law enforcement. She recognizes one Sheriff's deputy, a guy named Rudy, who let her off on a warning for speeding a few months back.

Deputy Rudy looks down at where O looks up at him.

She stirs with fear and fury.

He picks up her shotgun and examines it with appreciation.

"Be better if you just stay right there, ma'am," the cop tells her. "Pretty gun you got here. Nice wood."

What little ease his cadence brings to her concerning her own wellbeing, she feels nothing but the cold grip of horror as she watches Dahl draw his pistol and step toward the hallway.

The boom of Dahl's rugged, country voice cuts through the house as he shouts, "I told you to stay in them woods!"

Sean sits on the edge of the bed cradling their baby girl and looking at the closed door. Kat lies still in the bed beside them. It seems the pulses, the quakes, have subsided for the time being.

Sean considers what is left of this family.

This story.

This tragedy.

What is next?

What is left?

Dahl is stomping through the house, maybe in the kitchen now. The only thing he will find in there is the pitiful remnants of their simple meal.

Sean opens and closes his fist around the object in his closed hands: the vial meant to take his wife's life.

What is next?

What is left?

Family photos and trinkets decorate the walls and nooks of O's home. Dahl neglect to take in their stories as he nears the bedroom doors.

He stands with a gun in one hand, and the other touches a door's nob. It opens, slowly framing Dahl in its center.

The bed is neatly made, but the room is lived in. Homey.

A dog bed for Raphael is scooted into the corner.

"I'm not really into this game anymore!" Dahl yells.

Behind Dahl, another door slowly opens. Sean appears behind him.

"I wish it was a game," Sean says.

Dahl turns slowly, menacingly, his mouth curling into a scowl.

The young man who stands at the door of the bedroom across the hall looks haunted. He's broken down. Tired. Worn thin.

"I wish it was all pretend," Sean tells him.

Over Sean's shoulder, Dahl can see where Kat lies in bed. She's kicked the covers off, the evidence of the night's cruelty apparent.

In his arms, Sean holds their baby. Her little face peaks out from under the little blanket. Dahl begins to raise his weapon from where it hangs forgotten at his side, but Sean holds out the baby for him to take.

The baby.

So still. So very still.

Sean's eyes.

The exhaustion. The pain. The loss.

It doesn't take long for even Dahl to understand the situation and whatever fervor is left within him sags along with his gun.

"It's not pretend," Sean says, holding the child out.

He doesn't present her as a prop or a weapon but genuinely offers this man, this stranger, this person mad with violence towards him, to receive her into his arms as the child she is.

A child to be cherished.

"It's real. And … it's bigger than whatever this is you're trying to achieve. It's bigger than her. Me. You. Your friend. And I'm sorry – "

"It won't stop!" Dahl gives into his fear. "She won't. She's … dangerous. You know it. You've seen it. Look what she's – "

"You think she's the only one out there? This … isn't going to stop. This is just the start."

Sean cradles his baby girl, snuggling her to his chest.

From down the hall, O asks, "Sean?! Are you OK?!"

"You're right, though," Sean tells Dahl. "But she can't stop what is happening any more than you or I can stop that thing up there. I'm sorry, truly sorry. We're all scared, and nobody wanted this."

Dahl looks into Sean's eyes, into his arms, and at the burdened young woman over his shoulder.

"Sean?" O yells again.

The hard-looking man weighs his response.

Sean realizes he's been holding his breath as he watches Dahl safeties his pistol and tucks it back into the holster on his waist.

"No worries, Miss O," Sean yells down the hall. "How 'bout you?"

"Been worse!" she yells back.

The two men look at each other in the hallway for a moment longer. Dahl exits with nothing else to say.

Sean watches him walk back up the hall, the frenetic energy of vengeance sapped from him.

Miss O nurses her arm on the couch. She watches as Dahl walks by, his rough face not so much as glancing in her direction.

"We're done here," the man tells the gang that's gathered on O's couch.

She watches him walk out the broken door. The rest of the men file out behind him. Deputy Rudy is last. He does look apologetic as he pulls the busted door closed. Then, awkwardly, it drifts back open.

O's expression betrays her unbelief at the whole scenario that she just lived through.

"Hell of a night, huh, boy?" she asks Raphael.

The little Pekingese scratches at his collar, oblivious.

FIFTEEN

Sean tenderly places their swaddled baby girl in her basket. He tucks the blanket around her, taking great care to place the tiny bundle of dried flowers over her small chest. It is the best he can do.

His eyes take in his daughter one last time, attempting to memorize every detail of her little features. Even now, in the dim glow of the candles, he can see them both represented in her little face.

His furrowed, worried scrunch of a brow.

Her slight lips that smile *that* smile.

Who would she look like more, given enough time?

The basket's lid closes just like the possibility of answering that unbearably unanswerable question. Sean places it beside the bed where Kat sleeps. Her breath is shallow, pulse thready. She looks thin. Not simply slight, but translucent. Disappearing.

Behind their lids, her eyes chase after dreams. Or nightmares. Sean hopes for the first as he wipes a damp rag across her cheeks. He dabs at the blood dried at the turn of her nose.

On the nightstand, the vial of sedative sits ignored.

"What do you need, honey?" Miss O asks as she enters. She closes the door behind her. "What can I do?"

"Ask me again sometime."

As O joins them on the bed, she tenderly puts one hand on Sean's knee. Her other finds Kat's, which lays on top of the comforter.

"There's no way I can take this pain from you," she says. "At least I can help you carry it a little longer."

"I didn't tell her," Sean tells himself just as much as he speaks the words to O. "I never told her, but I think I like Josie. It's short for Josephine. I don't know what it means, but … but it's pretty."

"It is a lovely name," O assures him.

He watches as her aging hand stroke Kat's much younger but weaker-looking fingers.

"What am I going to do, O?" he asks.

"Ask me again sometime," she says.

Sean looks at his wife. He touches her hair. Her face. He can feel their goodbye approaching.

Without giving too much attention to the drama playing way overhead, Dahl gives the farmhouse one last look as he climbs up and into the cab of his big truck.

The living room door stands completely open, swinging on its hinges. Raphael barks contently at the men from the safety of the porch.

Dahl signals the rest of the fellas to load up and head out. He shoves the truck into gear. His engine sputters; fails to catch. Gauges flutter.

Through his windshield, he watches as every light in the house, every flood light on the property, every lamppost, and every decorative fixture sparks to life.

His truck lurches, revs, and flashes to life on its own.

In the sky, the heavens open.

Once again, the buzz and rattle of lightbulbs in lamps and fixtures can barely contain the energy pulsing through them.

Sean stands, watching as the vial on the small table rattles. It threatens to fall to the floor, shattering, but on instinct, he scoops it up at the last second. It feels heavy in his hand.

O is still on the bed holding her hand when Kat's chest arches violently toward the ceiling as if pulled by an invisible cable, ratcheting her skyward. The whole house is rocked; another pulse accompanies her next spasm. Finally, the lightbulbs detonate, overwhelmed by the energy that courses through them and everything else.

Sean and O are hurled to opposite ends room along the shockwave of Kat's tremor.

Sean hits the wall hard. His head connects with the floor as he crumples to the ground. His eyes lose focus, failing to rectify and consolidate his vision to a singular image.

He can make out at least two Miss O's struggling to their feet. He watches as she wipes her nose with the back of her hand. The nosebleed she's troubled with isn't going to be dammed so easily. Instead, it dribbles down to her blouse, flowering bright red.

Sean watches, woozy on the floor, his feet uncooperative, as O uses the bed's footboard to stand. She's trying to get to Kat but struggling. Ultimately, she falls back to the floor.

He looks to the bed at his wife's body, levitating no less than a foot off the bed. The covers slide off her body as she rises.

The farmhouse groans, shaking and shuddering as it is pulled apart one nail, one screw, one fastener, one piece here and there at a time.

Like moving through waist-high waters against an invisible current, Sean makes it to his feet and plods deliberately toward the bed. He swats at the tickle on his face, and the back of his hand comes away bloody. He tries to speak, yell, or scream, but it's like being squeezed from the inside and outside simultaneously.

All he can do to focus on one footstep and one breath at a time.

His hand reaches for Kat's. He's almost there …

When their fingers finally connect, her eyes snap open!

Instead of the soft hue of the eyes, he's gazed so intentionally and longingly into over the best years of his life that there's nothing left but indescribable otherness. No one looks back at him from behind that pure, terrifying power.

O has made it to the other side of the bed somehow. She reaches for Kat's wrist.

Sean can do nothing to stop it as tendrils of light leach from Kat. Her mouth opens as if in agony as they wrap around, entangling themselves with Miss O's shocked face and rigid body. Then, in a replay that still haunts him, Sean watches helpless and horrified as Miss O's body shudders, spine pulled erect as she's lifted off her feet.

O looks from Kat to Sean. It's not terror, confusion, or anger frozen on the woman's face but deep sadness. Sorrow. Pity. She trembles once more before, in an instant, she unceremoniously disintegrated.

Sean is stunned.

O is gone. Gone!

In sheer panic, he recoils and skids across the floor toward the door as his wife unfurls from the bed, untethered to gravity. Barely contained in any kind of physical form, she's nearly pure energy now. Yet, at the same time, she always has been.

All around them, the thin veil of the known is torn asunder. Localized reality is being undone. Things pop in and out of existence, entangling and disentangling on a quantum level at random.

A chunk of the roof above them is ripped off as Sean backpedals. His own feet threaten to trip him as he moves away from her; everything inside of him is yelling at him to escape.

To leave her behind.

To leave *them* behind.

The basket!

It still rests on the floor just by the bed, but that's across the room now. As dust and debris swirl around Sean, his thoughts are pulled like taffy. To retrieve their child would mean getting close to her again.

It doesn't matter.

Sean doesn't get to weigh his options or risk reaching for the basket. No, he is forced to watch in horror as the basket holding their child, their beautiful baby girl, is absorbed in that spiraling, chaotic light.

There … then gone!

With only a moment to think, Sean scrambles out of the bedroom, down the hall, and outside.

Something out of this world: a gaping maw of cosmic light swirls over the farmhouse! From the vortex at its center, chaotic daggers of lightning flash. They strike the ground, a pummeling rhythm.

Sean stands frozen on the porch.

Anything not secured to something solid defies gravity, hovering at different elevations seemingly randomly above the earth.

Miss O's classic of a pickup rotates on some invisible axis a solid forty feet in the air.

Several of the vehicles in Dahl's party that didn't make it off the property before the climax of this solar tantrum find themselves in a similar predicament, trapped in the wake of the incomprehensible.

A jagged bolt erupts from the cosmic storm, striking the house. What's left of the roof splinters as the concussion rocks the foundation and shatters windows. Above, the ceiling of the porch groans.

Sean ducks into the yard just as half of it caves in. He runs for what's left of the barn, with nowhere else to go, squeezing between gaps in the doors. He doesn't even try to pull them shut behind them. Following the path O had just led him on, he makes his way to Peter's office as fast as possible.

The structure shakes, threatening to either come down at once or take off into space whenever the time is right.

He sinks to the floor with his back against the old desk. Against the ceiling, instruments, pens, and other paraphernalia clatter, trying to get out. This is insanity.

The light from the sky, from the house, from *her*, from all around, those coils of radiation begin to ebb through the cracks in the old planks. They reach out to him. There is no escape, so he closes his eyes against it and waits for it to end. He squeezes them tight. So tight.

There, in the darkness that only exists behind his clenched lids, the rattle and raucous of everything else grows dim. There, in that place, a voice in his mind.

If you ever stop looking for me...

There along that stretch of farmland. Kat's head is on his chest.

"If you ever stop looking for me, no matter what you find," she said. A day ago. A lifetime ago.

His dream. Her drowned face.

No matter what you find.

Through clenched eyelids, her voice echoes.

Sean opens his eyes. The light through the cracks in the barn looks like daybreak. He fights to his feet resolved and without hesitation. Faces it. Faces her. Hovering between the house and the barn, Sean looks up at his wife, suspended a dozen feet above the ground.

With every step toward her, he can feel something more fundamental than his body and bones. Something somewhere at the source of all he is begins to give way. To unravel.

All around him, opaque images of their life. What was and what could have been. Memories both lived and imagined, experienced and hoped for. Beckoning him, something like letting go, like going home.

Sean stands before Kat, looking up into her eyes.

"I'll always find you," he tells her.

As a final quantum wake pulses from Kat's body, Sean's surprised scream is inaudible as he is irrevocably undone.

SUNFLOWER

Waking and drifting off again,
like a dream caught hanging in predawn stillness.

Some primordial echo reverberates.
A song at the center of existence.

This kaleidoscopic unfolding contains the meaning of everything
and answers to one name

Beauty.

This spirit, this soul.
Always being and always becoming.

Blooming.

Sinking deeper into beautiful truth:
We are never alone.

SUNFLOWER

SIXTEEN

Miraculously, one barn door remains attached. It swings open on its large hinges as dawn breaks over the farm. What's left of the farmhouse, which isn't much, stands against the receding cosmic winds.

Raphael barks at the indescribable morning, unscathed, standing on what's left of the front porch.

Dahl's truck lays on its roof. Inside, life stirs in the man's bloodied face, eyes opening; the left shot through with blood from broken vessels.

The lean man forces himself to crawl through the shattered rear window. Rolling onto his back, he accumulates a fair number of cuts squeezing out from underneath the truck's bed. No matter. There's only one way.

His head and torso are finally freed, and Dahl squints against the morning sun, taking a few deep breaths. He winces at the pain that radiates through his chest. Still, a laugh tickles his inside and gurgles up, escaping through his busted lips. This subtle sign of victory and gratitude. He made it.

But when he opens his eyes, there it is. Though receding, beyond the clouds, something rumbles and rolls and moves.

Alive.

Astral.

Ominous.

Inescapable.

Lovely.

SUNFLOWER

SUNFLOWER

AUTHOR'S NOTE

Stories have always been important to me. Stories and storytelling have been many things for me: an easy means of escaping reality, a pressure release valve, and – if I'm honest – stories have helped with a lot of the emotional heavy lifting throughout my life.

I often spend more time in my head than in the real world. There are constant conversations, constant observation, and constant creation swirling in my mind.

Sunflower was challenging a story to write. I wanted to lean into my fears during the early days of the Covid-19 pandemic, but I didn't expect to go on the journey I did while crafting this little book.

Thank you for sitting through this extended counseling session with me. I'll save some room on the couch for you next time too.

Charlottesville, VA
2022

SUNFLOWER

Made in the USA
Columbia, SC
24 November 2022

71733820R00076